T0086374

BEYOND

THE MIRACLE

RANGE

BEYOND
⊣ THE MIRACLE ⊢
RANGE

ELLIOTT UNDERWOOD

BEYOND THE MIRACLE RANGE

This is a work of fiction. All of the characters, names, incidents, organizations, and dialogue in this novel are either the products of the author's imagination or are used fictitiously.

iUniverse books may be ordered through booksellers or by contacting:

iUniverse
1663 Liberty Drive
Bloomington, IN 47403
www.iuniverse.com
844-349-9409

Because of the dynamic nature of the Internet, any web addresses or links contained in this book may have changed since publication and may no longer be valid. The views expressed in this work are solely those of the author and do not necessarily reflect the views of the publisher, and the publisher hereby disclaims any responsibility for them.

Any people depicted in stock imagery provided by Getty Images are models, and such images are being used for illustrative purposes only. Certain stock imagery © Getty Images.

ISBN: 978-1-6632-2322-7 (sc)
ISBN: 978-1-6632-2323-4 (e)

Library of Congress Control Number: 2021909823

Print information available on the last page.

iUniverse rev. date: 05/13/2021

CONTENTS

SYNOPSIS

Chapter One – Seamus Todd walks in on a hostage situation in his own cozy lighthouse. He escapes to warn the ambassador.

Chapter Two – The ambassador, Michael Desmond and his entourage travel to Babylon in an airship (fossil fuels having been spent centuries ago.) Michael is injured by an assassination attempt, leaving his protegee in charge.

Chapter Three – Seamus Todd tries to fit into the chaotic bustle of the Tower of Babylon and finds himself on trial for a crime he didn't commit.

Chapter Four – Our hero finds himself married.

Chapter Five – He is tortured to death at Pryadar's command but gets better.

Chapter Six – He gets revenge on Pryadar.

Chapter Seven – He is exiled for speaking up for the deposed Emperor. He and the Emperor depart together.

INTRODUCTION

"Between the Elves and the Asuras exists a state of perpetual war, as long as day follows night, and night follows day. And unless you destroy us, we will never stop killing you."

Ravana I, first Asura King

The year is 5525 of the Fifth Age. When the Perpetual War heated up again between the Elves and the Asuras, Sean McKenzie and many other Elves were called away to war. His wife, Caroline, moved herself and her three youngest from the capital to a lighthouse on the southern coast of Ireland, vowing to keep the lantern lit until the war ended. Her youngest son, Seamus Todd, went with them.

The Fifth Age began when the Alien Poids invaded Earth. Under pressure, Mankind split into several daughter races, including the Elves, Kachinas, Amazons, Ethiopians, Easterners, Southerners, and Genies. The descendants of the Aliens were the Demons and the Asuras. The Asuras, though few, hold most of the power and are considered royalty, and even divinity. The Demons, who are bred to believe the Asuras are gods, are second in the hierarchy, and are superior to the Genies. The Genies form the third caste. At the bottom, and most numerous, are the Zombies, the undead who enforce the Asura's reign in the dreaded Regime.

Seamus Todd McKenzie was digging up potatoes when he saw the light go out. He'd been thinking about the Elven hostages in the Regime, when suddenly the light house was dark. He wondered what it meant. He already had dug enough potatoes, so he decided to hurry home and see what the darkened light meant. If all was well, it meant the War was over.

CHAPTER ONE

Beyond the Miracle Range
Blowing Smoke

Stunning

    Sprite Elves have the ability to stun with their hands. A circle of cells on their dominant hand can be used whenever they are in danger. Their DNA was reconstructed with strands from butterflies, eagles, and jellyfish to give them wings, keen eyesight, and the stinging ability. Their actual name for themselves is Tuatha, but they so resemble Elves from Celtic and Nordic myth that they have identified themselves as an Elvish people.

He burst in the door and found a terrorist in his home. The terrorist was still there when he turned off the light.

Now, normally there was no terrorist in the McPherson lighthouse. Seamus Todd had just been in the far field, gathering potatoes from their victory garden. He stepped into the mud room and turned on the light and there was the terrorist. So, he turned the light off but of course that did no good. He was looking down the barrel of a gun. The man grabbed him and forced him into the golden light of what was usually a warm and cozy kitchen.

There were six other people there. Three Elves, his mom, his sisters, Siobhan and Shannon. And three more invaders.

"Is anybody else coming?"

"No one," said Caroline McKenzie, his mom. "He's only my son. He's just a boy."

Seamus Todd looked at the figure who had spoken, and a chill ran down his spine. It was a demon. His skin was fierier than the fiercest sunburn, he had horns and spikes instead of hair and a beard, and his eyes were bright yellow. Unlike the others, his dress seemed Egyptian, with a nemes headdress with a cobra on it, and wrapped like a mummy below his jeweled collar. The others appeared to be Genies. They were dressed in Middle Eastern style, long gold robes with headdresses, except one who sported a blue turban.

"How old are you, boy?"

"Fourteen," he said.

"Why isn't he in the army?"

"He's not old enough," said his mother.

"He would be if he were on our side."

"Well, I want him here with me, where he's safe."

"Ironic," the demon snorted. "Sit at the table."

He was about to say no, when his mother interrupted.

"We were just about to have dinner. Why don't we serve you, and then you gentlemen can – be on your way."

The women served the men, which he understood was how things happened where they came from. There was roast leg of lamb with mint jelly, golden potatoes, peas in white sauce, and chocolate cake.

"This is the most delicious lamb I've ever tasted," said the one in the turban. He somehow seemed nicer than the others.

"It's not real meat, but vegetable made to taste like meat," Seamus Todd explained.

"You're kidding."

"I don't kid about food."

"Now, Seamus Todd, we must show our guests the hospitality of the Celtic Elves."

"I notice you always call him Seamus Todd. Do all young Elves use two names?"

"No. When he was little, the only way to get his attention was to use his full name. So, we just always call him Seamus Todd."

"Do you Elves drink beer?" Asked the Demon.

"We do. I'll get you some."

She returned with four mugs of beer.

"Mom, can I have some?"

"Don't be silly, dear. You're still a little boy. Beer is for our guests."

The girls were glancing surreptitiously at the beards of the men, since male Elves only grow beards after they were fourteen hundred years old. The men of the Regime always wore beards. Besides dress, and pointed ears, and the fact that the Elves have antennas, it was a quick way to see which team they were on.

"I might not get another chance," Seamus Todd said what everybody else at the table was trying not to have said.

She served the foaming mugs, and as they drank, she asked the Demon, "Men of the Regime, what brings you to Ireland? Do you have any news of the war?"

"Especially the fifth company," said Siobhan. "That's where our dad is stationed."

"We're not regular army, so we wouldn't know the enemy positions. And if I did, I wouldn't tell you."

"Why are you here, then?"

"Your queen is in the vicinity, isn't she?"

"Why, yes. We were just about to get ready to go see her when you gentlemen showed up on the doorstep."

"She's meeting Michael Desmond tonight?"

"Yes."

"Our orders are to kill her, and as many Elves as we can tonight. And not be taken alive."

Caroline paled, Siobhan's hand went to her mouth, and Shannon looked like she might cry. Seamus Todd determined not to react.

"You're a suicide squad. You're yellow robes."

"That's right."

"But what about your own lives? Surely, that must mean something to you," said Caroline.

"Not compared to the crown of martyrdom."

"Please," said Siobhan. Queen Margaret is our. . ."

"Your what?"

"A good queen. Our good queen."

Mom was trying to act like everything was normal, and Siobhan was following along. Shannon, though, the younger sister, seemed on the verge of tears and was eating with difficulty. Suddenly, her eyes bulged and she reached for the water.

"She's choking." Seamus Todd ran to her side and lifted her left arm. That seemed to help, and she got the bite down. Her eyes were full of tears now, but she said "I'm all right. I'm all right."

They would have just let her choke to death, he thought bitterly.

"Seamus Todd, why don't you get your tablet and play our guests some music?"

"All right. I'll go get it."

He headed up the spiral staircase into the lighthouse, where his little room was tucked away, just under the light room. The second he was out of sight, he pressed nine nine nine on his watch.

"Nine nine nine, what is your emergency?"

"There are terrorists in our home, the McPherson lighthouse."

"Someone can be there from Dublin by air car in ten minutes. Don't hang up the phone."

"Where is that boy?" Roared the demon.

"I have to. I have to go." He looked up to see a pale, frightened boy, hiding in his room. Blond and blue eyed. Himself. In the mirror.

He turned off the watch, knowing they would call again, grabbed a green tablet off his dresser and hurried back downstairs.

"Here I am."

The Demon looked at him like he knew he had made a phone call but said nothing.

He began to play. Like most Elves, he had a very good singing voice, and though his wasn't considered the best in his class, his voice was good enough. As he sang, the tablet began to pick up the song. He sang of sunshine, and light began to glow in the room. He sang of the forest, and trees appeared, intertwining the beams of the kitchen. He sang of a river through the forest, and the water appeared. He sang of birds and deer, and they became visions. He sang of mountains, and the mountains shimmered in the distance.

While he sang, he looked around for ideas on how to defeat them. Most promising was his father's huge old rifle over the mantelpiece, though there was no way he could reach it without being noticed. He could hardly take them out with his mother's copper pots. Elves could stun with a touch, but it would be difficult to get all of them at once. As long as the intruders had guns, they had the advantage.

"Dance with me." One of them grabbed Siobhan and whirled her around the room in a mockery of dance.

Seamus Todd began to lose control. Dark figures appeared in his vision, and they bore more than a passing resemblance to the invaders. The shadows grew, and the forest began to splinter apart, and darkness boiled up and overcame the vision. Seamus Todd stopped singing.

"Enough," the demon waved his hand through the picture. "Do you think I don't know what you're doing?"

"I'm trying to get you to spare me and my family," said Caroline.

"We'll need one of you to take us to the castle."

"I will," said Seamus Todd at once.

"Not you. We need one of the women."

"What about the rest of us?" Asked Mom.

"We have no further need for you," said the Demon

"I'll go," said Siobhan.

Seamus Todd felt his mind growing calm, as he waited to see what happened. He looked at each of the three women in his family, as if trying to fix them in his mind. Mom, with her light blonde hair and green cameo. Siobhan, with her dark good looks and red and black shawl. Shannon, with her blond hair and green eyes that matched her dress.

"You, boy."

"Yes."

The Demon took off his boots and slid them across the floor.

"Clean my boots, boy."

"No."

"Clean those boots."

"No. Next, he'll make us dig our own graves."

"Please, Seamus Todd, just do what he asks," said his mother.

"I will not clean those boots." He faced the Demon, hands on hips. "Clean them yourself."

The Demon's only response was to backhand Seamus Todd, so the boy slammed onto the floor. He still didn't clean the boots. The fiend turned on Caroline. "How would you like to pick in which order you watch your children die?"

"Please, don't." She spread her arms as if she could protect her children from bullets that way.

Yeah, don't, thought Seamus Todd desperately. I think we all know which one she would start with.

"You Elves. You're the most arrogant race ever to appear on this planet. You. . ."

"We are not." He was on his feet and about to say more but his mother grabbed him from behind and slipped her hand over his mouth.

Mom said, "I think you are attributing your own crimes to us."

"All the resources wasted, centuries gone past, in order to bring your people to heel," said the Demon.

"Whose fault is that?" His Mother said. "You seek to destroy our people, but you haven't been able to."

"Well, the final solution is already set up. Why can't you Elves see reason and simply stop resisting?"

"The reason for your planned genocide?"

"How dare you!"

"It's the truth."

Mom squeezed his shoulder as she let him go. "Get to the castle if you can," she whispered.

"Could I grab a smoke, boss?" Asked the Genie in the blue turban.

"Can I go with him?" Seamus Todd saw his chance.

"You know I don't like your smoking," admonished his mother.

"Can I?" He faced the Demon. "Consider it a last request. One isn't going to kill me."

"Go ahead," he snorted. "But if you try to escape, we kill you and your family."

He followed the blue turbaned Genie out into the cool night air. It had rained recently, and the night was pleasantly cool. The stars were trying to come out overhead, though it was partly cloudy. He saw their vehicle behind the house. How could he have missed it?

The terrorist lit a cigarette for the boy, then his own. Seamus Todd began coughing.

The terrorist pounded him on the back. "Are you sure you know how to smoke, boy?"

"Oh, yes," he coughed. As a matter of fact, he'd never even seen a cigarette before, much less smoked one.

"What is that?" Asked the terrorist. Seamus Todd was pretty sure this was a pretext to getting a bullet in the back of his head, but he looked anyway. In the distance, a large animal was coming across the meadow.

"That's an Irish Elk," he explained. "He's one of the creatures Elf scientists have been able to bring back from extinction."

"What a trophy he'd make."

"Is that all you can see?"

"Of course not. I see a large sack of meat."

Seamus Todd got closer to the Genie while he was talking, and suddenly blew smoke in his face. While he was distracted, Seamus Todd touched him with his stinging hand. The guy fell like a sack of meat. Seamus Todd helped lower him to the ground, and then he was off and running as fast as he could.

He jumped the stone fence and headed toward the nearest village, a mile away.

Something was coming up behind him. He looked back, but it was only the Irish Elk. "What's the matter, boy? Do you want to help me?"

He led the giant creature to the stone wall so he could clamber up on its back without startling it. A loud sound came from the lighthouse, and again. Gunshots. He wanted to race back and find out if his family still survived, but he remembered his mother's request. Maybe her final request before she died. So, he leaned forward on the deer, and held on tight. He could smell the faint scent of its sweat. They were off. The night sped over them with the sound of galloping hooves. The lights of the village appeared, twinkling.

He turned on his watch and called emergency again.

"We're on our way. We should be there in three minutes."

It wasn't cold, but his teeth were chattering. "I'm outside. I'm almost to Cor."

The friendly neighborhood tavern awaited him, the glow of its windows welcoming.

"Thanks, boy," he slipped to the ground, petted the animal and let it go. Then he dashed into the tavern. The dark interior was only lit by some glowing bulbs. Most of those present were Elves. Out of breath, he gasped, "Terrorists – the lighthouse."

"That's Sean's boy," said one.

Another caught him, as he staggered. "Take it easy, lad."

"Heading to Michael Desmond's. We have to warn him." Seamus Todd said.

"Hold on. We'll call the castle."

They gave him a drink of water while he caught his breath and told them all what was happening. The circle of Elves grew tight around him as he explained what happened.

9

In a moment, a car arrived, and an Elf lady with dark red hair dashed in. Like all Elves, she was very beautiful, but her face was flushed. Her lovely long ears pointed down instead of up. "I'm Erin Macomber, lord Desmond's aid. Who's trying to kill Ambassador Desmond?"

"There are terrorists at my house, they say they're going to kill Queen Margaret. And maybe Lord Desmond, as well."

She just looked at him. *She doesn't believe me.* Thought Seamus Todd. *Why doesn't she believe me?*

"How do you know what their plans are?"

"They told us."

"And you got away from them? How?"

"I stunned one of them and my mom told me to run. Please, why don't you believe me?"

"Were they yellow robes?"

"Yes, they were a suicide squad."

"How do you know?"

"They said so."

"All right. Get in the air car. We'll head back to warn the ambassador."

They took off. Erin didn't speak or look at him for the short trip. He wondered if she still really didn't believe him or if she was just worried about what was happening. She ran her fingers through her long red hair and twisted it. She saw him watching her and stopped, embarrassed.

When they got there, he pointed out the Terrorist's vehicle. He followed her into the castle, past the startled guards, blew through the reception line, and scrambled into the main hall. The place was huge, made of stone, and covered in tapestries. He saw Siobhan, followed by two men in long robes. The terrorists.

"Siobhan," he yelled, startling several people, including himself.

She turned and looked at him, but there was no look of recognition in her face. Was she drugged, or hypnotized?

The Demon ripped out of his robes, snarling. The Elves scrambled to get out of his way.

Erin ran up to him and screamed. The Demon and the Genie were both lifted off their feet and smashed into the wall. She's a Banshee, he realized.

The Demon recovered himself, squatting like a giant red toad, and leaped out the nearest window in a spray of shattering glass. The Genie sprawled on the floor as two guards surrounded him. He wasn't going anywhere.

Siobhan collapsed to the floor. He ran to her and cradled her in his arms, like he would have been too embarrassed to do if she was conscious. "Siobhan, Siobhan."

Someone came up behind him, someone in a white gown. "Grandma."

The Queen said, "Seamus Todd, she's going to be all right. The ambulance is on its way."

"She's cold."

Queen Margaret knelt down beside him and took the girl's hand. Her face was unlined, and only her eyes showed her great age.

"She's got a pulse."

"Is she going to be all right?"

"I think so, dear."

He held onto her hand until the paramedics came and followed the stretcher to the ambulance. He finally let her go.

"Seamus Todd, come with us." He followed the Queen into Desmond's office, where he was waiting to talk to them.

Michael Desmond was old, even for an Elf. His skin was so pale it was almost transparent, and his long hair was white. He was sitting behind his desk, but he rose and gravely took the boy's hand.

"Thank you, lad. You saved me, the queen, and maybe a bunch of other people."

"I talked with your mom. Everything's all right," said the queen.

"But I heard gunshots."

"Your mom fired into the air. When they followed you outside, she grabbed the gun and locked the door. She and Shannon are just fine."

"They were going to kill us all."

"They were going to kill us," he repeated. It hit him, just like that.

"You're safe now. Everybody's safe. It's all right."

"Oh, good." He sagged onto the desk.

"You were about to tell me why you came, your majesty?" Said Michael Desmond.

The Queen said, "Blake and I want you to go to the Regime and negotiate for the hostages."

Seamus Todd had heard about the hostage situation, of course, but hadn't really paid it a lot of attention. But then, he'd never known what it was like to be held hostage, either.

"I'm retired," said Michael Desmond.

"I know you are, but I bring the pleading of all the Elves to take up one last mission. It would mean a great deal to the king and me, and your income certainly won't suffer," the queen offered.

"I don't know."

"I'm afraid there's more at stake than a diplomatic mission." She sounded a little desperate. "If you don't come, he's said he will undertake a vendetta against you. We've seen the reach he has. We know he can do it. Tonight, might have been a warning."

"Well, when you put it that way, how can I say no?"

"Is there anything I can do to help?" Seamus Todd asked.

"Do you need an aide along, Michael?"

"I might have need of a translator. Can you speak Persian, Lad?"

"No, but I can learn."

"I don't know. The mission might be dangerous."

"I'm sure I'll be all right as long as I'm with you."

"He's obviously your grandson. But we might be dealing with Pryadar himself."

Pryadar, thought Seamus Todd. We're going to face Pryadar the Spider?

"I'm not afraid of Pryadar." Said Seamus Todd.

"Aren't you?"

"No."

"Then it's possible you don't understand the situation."

"I've met Pryadar. I know he can be difficult," said Margaret. "He has a heart of gold."

For some reason, maybe the way she said it, it sounded odd. But then, among the Elves, a heart of gold meant something cold and artificial.

Seamus Todd said, "I don't think we should look down on him just because he's an Asura," indignantly.

"It's not because he's an Asura."

"Pryadar is mentally unstable," said Michael.

"Maybe he just hasn't been exposed enough to Elves to learn about us."

"He's been exposed. He's been exposed."

Seamus Todd asked, "has he ever killed anyone?"

"He doesn't have to kill people himself," Michael explained. "As virtual ruler of the Regime, he doesn't have to put on his own jack boots personally. He has it done."

"Well, I think we can persuade him to let the hostages go."

"Diplomat."

"Quick on his feet, too," said Margaret.

"All right, my boy, you can come along. As you were saying, your majesty."

"So, you'll do it?"

"Of course, I'll do it, your majesty."

"Then that's all settled. Maybe you should go check on your sister?"

"Siobhan! Of course. I've got to get to the hospital. Which one did they take her to?"

"The one in Cor, sweetie."

"I've got to go. Goodbye."

As he was leaving, he overheard the queen say, "you know what to do if he won't negotiate, don't you, lord Desmond."

"Yes, your majesty."

What were they talking about? The boy wondered. Did their side engage in intrigue and assassination like the other side did? He decided to find out more later.

At the end of summer, the Perpetual War, which had been simmering for fifty centuries, flared up again. Harsha, the old Emperor, was failing, and his son, Pryadar, had taken over most of the functions of the government. A peaceful protest in the province of Persia had been met with violence. The king and queen of Tuatha had sent a polite but strongly worded protest over the whole affair. Pryadar's reply had been war. Twice he sent a space armada to attack Tuatha, but the Elf fleet was able to defeat it both times. The Regime had then raided the Elvish embassy and taken ten hostages. Pryadar also assembled the largest army in history. Four billion zombies and various other troops were making their way across Europe. The Elves were bracing for the largest war in history, and it was very likely one they were going to lose. Through the long years of attrition, their population had come close to dropping to below sustainable levels. Their population was less than three million, and they couldn't afford another disastrous loss.

Erin was giving him a ride. She was a good deal more relaxed and friendly now, though not a great deal more talkative. Perhaps she just wasn't all that outspoken. But she smiled at him, and she was beautiful when she smiled. Now he was the one who was focused on his mission, and she was calm.

When he got to the hospital, they directed him to the emergency room. Mom and Shannon met him in the waiting room, and they all hugged each other.

"I'm so glad my whole family is safe," said Caroline. "They said Siobhan is going to be all right."

"Can we see her?"

"Soon."

"Mom, I got a job."

"You did?"

"As a translator for Michael Desmond. We're going to New Babylon."

She smiled, but her eyes did not.

"What about school?"

"Traveling is educational."

"What about Doug?" Doug was his best friend at school.

"He'll be all right," said Seamus Todd.

"What about your chores at home? Who's going to do them?"

"Ask the girls to do it."

"You know they won't."

"Well," he let a little venom slip. "Then they won't get done."

"Dear, we moved out here to escape palace life and the easy, push button world."

"No, Mom, you moved us out here to escape the push button world. I like living in the modern world."

"You saw today what the modern world can do."

15

"Yes, because we weren't prepared. If we had had a security system like most people, they wouldn't have gotten in in the first place."

"The Asuras are dangerous. Seamus Todd, they can't be trusted."

"Mom, that's not fair." You can't group people like that, he thought. There are lots of good Genies, there are even some good demons. Can't you stop being so judgmental?

"You haven't met any Asuras. I have."

"And you judge them by a few?"

"I judge them by their deeds. Pryadar is a very dangerous man. It's not that he's an Asura, it's who he is. Dangerous. A threat to free people everywhere, but especially us."

"I just don't believe someone can be evil."

"That's because you've never had to confront it. Evil is very real, Seamus Todd. It exists, and there are those who would destroy us."

"If we just talk to them. . ."

"Honey, I know what the Asuras want. They've said it themselves. They don't want to share the world with us. They want us dead."

"Emperor Harsha was a good Asura, you've said so yourself."

"Compared to Pryadar, he's a saint. He spent his reign preparing his kingdom for war. Now, Pryadar is reaching out for you, me, everybody."

"We shouldn't be afraid of Pryadar," said Seamus Todd.

"He swore Perpetual War, dear. He's not going to stop until we're all dead. I'm sure he's the one who sent the terrorists tonight."

"Then we shouldn't let him get away with it."

The nurse came in just then and asked, "would you like to see your daughter now?"

"Yes," they all said, so they followed her into the room.

Siobhan lay flat in bed, her black hair falling on either side of her pale face. She looked exhausted but peaceful. Caroline brushed her forehead. "We're here, sweetie."

She mumbled something inarticulate. They stayed for a while, until she fell into a restful sleep, and then they quietly slipped out.

"Do you really want to go to Babylon?"

"More than anything."

"I wanted to give you something," said mom as they returned to the waiting room. She took off a silver ring set with a piece of green stone. "Your father gave it to me when I told him you were going to be born."

"So, does this mean you're all right with me going?"

She didn't say anything.

Since it was a girl's ring, he would wear it on his chain, where he already had a Celtic cross.

They returned to the lighthouse for the night. Seamus Todd tried to go to sleep. He tossed and turned. Was the door locked? He wasn't even sure they had a lock. The problem had never come up before. He tried to dream of flying trains, but his mind kept returning to the presence of the terrorists. It was after three that he finally fell asleep, more from exhaustion than any ability to relax.

In the morning, the police dropped by to interview them. One by one, they met over the kitchen table.

When it was his turn, the male officer explained, "I'm Officer O'Toole, this is Officer Monaghan."

"Hi." Not off to a brilliant start.

"Tell us what happened last night."

"I came into the house and there were these guys here. They said they were from the Regime. Three Genies and a demon."

"What did they want?"

"They said they were here to kill the queen."

"They actually said that?"

"Their exact words were "Our orders are to kill her, and as many Elves as we can tonight.""

He described the invaders, the tense situation, the flight into the village, the dash to the castle, and what happened there.

"Where do you think he went when he got away?"

"I don't know. Probably home. That's where I'd go."

"Once a yellow robe leaves on a suicide mission, they don't come back."

"Which means they will probably try again."

"The queen and lord Desmond are both being guarded. We might have to put a detail on your family, too."

"I'm going with Michael Desmond."

"I see."

They visited for about forty-five minutes, but it was mostly repetitious, as they made him say the same things over again. Finally, they let him go and asked him to send in Shannon.

Seamus Todd wandered outside. Was that Michael's car hovering in the distance?

It was. Erin drew up beside him, and Michael lowered the dome.

"Good morning, lad. We were going to Cymri this morning and ask a giant if he wanted to go along as my bodyguard. Did you want to come along as well?"

"Sure. Let me tell my mom."

In a moment he was back and clambered into the back seat. Michael and his stone dog were waiting for him.

Stone dogs make perfect pets. When awake, they are courageous, loyal, and protective. When not needed, they turn to stone until stroked or called. They were an invention of Elvish science.

"What's his name?" Asked Seamus Todd as the dog crawled into his lap.

"Her name's Missy."

In less than thirty minutes, they were in Cardiff. This lovely town, with its stone houses and castles, was one of the most picturesque in the isles. They stopped at a gray stone house.

Brendan and Mrs. Penrod welcomed them in. Over tea and cherry cake, they discussed what they wanted him to do.

Giants are an offshoot of Elves. Born human size, they can grow as large as nine feet tall. Mister Penrod, or Brendan, as he said they could call him, was about seven foot five, not very tall for a giant.

While the adults talked, he looked around at their comfortable little house. Missy was on his lap, when she suddenly stiffened and began barking.

"What is it, girl?" He followed her to the door, which was surrounded by small diamond shaped windows that let him see the shadows of people approaching but not the details.

"Somebody's coming." He opened the door.

"Lord Desmond," said a voice he had never hoped to hear again. It was the demon from last night. He and another Genie were on the door step.

Seamus Todd slammed the heavy door shut, and he just had time to catch a glimpse of the demon's face as he jumped back.

The door slammed open again, with smoke curling around the edges. It fell on Seamus Todd, and he was trapped beneath the heavy door. His ears were ringing from the explosion. All was chaos, as he tried to get up. Brendan took one enormous hand and lifted it off him easily.

The beautiful room was filled with smoke and ash, but nobody seemed to be hurt except for Seamus Todd. In the distance, an ambulance wail sounded.

Erin took him to the ambulance. "Don't look at the bodies. It's not a pretty sight."

But he couldn't miss it. The genie who had been wearing the bomb was spattered all over the wall, the porch, the lawn, everywhere. The Demon lay very still under his heavy robes. Parts of his skin were showing and looked like it had already turned to rock.

They sat him down on the bumper of the ambulance and treated him for scratches and damaged ears. He was going to be all right, they assured him.

Lord Desmond came out. "You saved me again, lad."

He nodded, not able to say anything more. His nerves, he was afraid, were going into a permanent state of shock, and his paranoia was just beginning.

Brendan came out and said, "in conclusion, lord Desmond, I would be happy to come with you as a bodyguard. Apparently, you're going to need it."

Who did this?"

"Who do you think? Pryadar."

"Why would he send assassins after somebody he was trying to invite?"

"Pryadar's crazy," said Erin. "We don't know why he does things. The orders must have come from different heads. But I think it was to send us a message."

"And that would be. . ."

"Do what I want you to do, or die."

"What does he want us to do?"

"Come to him willingly, I would guess."

"And I will," said Michael. "We'll leave for Paris tomorrow. But now I don't know if you going along is a good idea, lad. You could have been killed."

"I'm more determined than ever to go, sir. If you let me."

"I can get another translator."

"And risk their life?"

"You're only a boy."

"A boy who saved your life, twice. Don't you see, I have to go along, not just as a translator, but a bodyguard, too. I'm good luck."

"You have the scars to prove it. All right, Seamus Todd, you can come. But you must do exactly as I tell you to do."

"All right."

"I mean it, even if I tell you to save yourself and let the rest of us die."

"Yes."

"When we get to Paris, we'll use the language scanner at the university."

CHAPTER TWO
Journey to Babylon

The next day, the four arrived in Paris.

Paris was the largest city in Tuatha, with over five hundred thousand people. Though it had a much smaller population than it had at one time, it was still about the same size as its old dimensions, and filled with some of the most beautiful architecture in the world. Domed buildings stood upon pillars over green gardens, glittering in the sun. He saw at least a dozen castles or chalets on the way. Their first stop was the University of Paris. The oldest school still in existence, it was over six thousand years old. One of the beautiful buildings was the languages department. Inside was a device that looked like a cross between a silver spider and a laser cannon. They put Seamus Todd in front of it and zapped him.

It wasn't a way to instantly learn languages. He still had to study it like any language, but it made it much faster and easier to memorize.

They spent three days in Paris. Seamus Todd's favorite place to visit was the National Library. More than a trillion books, the largest collection in history, with scripts ranging cuneiform from ancient Sumerian and the Library at Alexandria to modern works. Since all Elves are gifted in the arts and sciences, they had many good writers, and a published author could make a very good living. Publishing was one of their largest industries.

The building was massive, domed green and white, and chock full of books. In truth however, there once had been more. The collection was breaking up, some to be sent to the island of Iceland, others to the eastern borders in the Nordic Peninsula. The zombie army was approaching, and Paris was certainly one of their main targets. While they were there, he saw air trucks pulling up to take another load away. It made him sad to think about it.

They also visited the plant where one eighth of the world's food was produced. There were six plants. Besides the one in Paris, there was one in the Iberian peninsula, one in the north of the Island of Great Britain, one in the province of Poland, one in Sweden, and one in New Berlin. There were also food producing regions in North and South America and China, but eighty percent of all food was produced by the Elves.

With a sound agricultural base, they managed many large industries, like movie production, mining and metal production, the largest and most advanced education system ever devised, (Elves spend more than half their fifteen hundred year lifespan going to school) and most of the world's art.

They visited several museums, including the expanded and rebuilt Louvre, ate at sidewalk cafes, and took in the night life. Everywhere Seamus Todd went, though, his books on Persian went with him. He studied as much as possible, even when they went to the opera. Dancing was the only time he put them down and showed what he could do. Seamus Todd might have only been a fair singer, but he was the best dancer in school. He danced with everyone who offered, and both men and women danced with him, as was the custom. Everyone agreed if it was a dance contest, he would have won. Instead, it was just a good night on the town. Then they would retire to their hotel rooms and sleep until the next day.

Seamus Todd still could hardly sleep. The home invasion haunted his dreams. There were also the hostages in Babylon to think about. Now that he had gone through a similar experience, he knew a little more of what they must be going through. Then there was the mad whirlwind that was Paris, the exciting places to see, the exotic night life. It was very different from his staid existence in the lighthouse. He was averaging a sleep of only four hours a night, and these were punctuated by nightmares.

After three days, their ride was ready. Seamus Todd read the brochure as they walked through the morning mist up the crowded Champs de Elyse. It seemed the whole city had turned out to see them. "The Globe is the largest airship ever built, thirteen hundred feet long by two hundred fifty feet wide, weighing two hundred ninety-two tons. It has designs of the continents on each side, and a gondola a thousand feet long. It has its own nuclear engine and was commissioned in 5509. Currently owned by the government for important missions, it has a crew of forty, including a chef. But wouldn't it be easier just to take a car?"

"Almost all of the country's energy, including running cars, is produced by our fusion reactor," explained Michael Desmond. "Clean, cheap, virtually limitless, we have to waste energy to keep it from becoming a burden. But it's range is only as far as the borders of Tuatha."

"We have ships that could get us there in five minutes," said Erin. "But you're not the only one who needs to do some work on the journey. We're gathering information about the enemy army."

"Oh, I should have known that." He decided not to be the first to say anything, lest he not act enough like a translator. He'd just be quiet and let the others lead.

They went up the gang plank. Everything was magnificent, made of carved wood, stained glass, marble, quartz. It put the most luxurious ocean liner to shame.

The most fascinating place to be was close to the pilot's room, a glass bottom observatory room, with a balcony outside with telescopes. Seamus Todd claimed it as his study and unloaded his books there. Then he went out to see the zeppelin take off.

Michael Desmond was at the top of the gang plank, thanking all of Paris for seeing them off and promising to recover the captives as quickly and safely as possible. "We'll be back with the hostages, no matter what," he promised. Seamus Todd wondered again about the 'no matter what.'

Then they were lifting off, above the fog and into the full light of the sun. He waved at the dwindling crowd for as long as he thought they could see him, then he went inside and opened a book. He was soon conjugating verbs.

Airships

are a common sight over the commonwealth of Tuatha. Though much slower than spaceships or airplanes, these luxurious floating castles have become the preferred mode of travel. Many receive power from the fusion device, and thus can only work inside the borders of Tuatha, but others, like the Globe, are equipped to travel between continents. Some are even stationary, serving as restaurants, museums, and other tourist attractions. The majority, however, are built for transportation. The Globe is the largest airship

---

ever built, dwarfing the Hindenburg and other ships from the first golden age of lighter than air travel.

Globe	Hindenburg
Thirteen hundred feet long	eight hundred twelve feet long
two hundred fifty feet in diameter	one hundred thirty-five feet in diameter
23,375,000 Cubic feet	7,063,000 Cubic feet
two hundred ninety-two tons	two hundred thirty five tons
Nuclear Powered	Gas Powered
Speed three hundred miles per hour	eighty-four miles per hour
Commissioned 5509 of the Fifth	1936 of the Fourth Age
Age, so it's sixteen years old	
Helium	Hydrogen

The fields and hills and forests of the French countryside rolled on below. Erin came in to check on him. "Am I seeing a pattern in the landscape?" He asked.

"Yes, McKenzie. They've been shaping a spiral for thousands of years. See how even the villages and monuments are incorporated in the design?" She always called him McKenzie, like an adult.

"Incredible."

They floated above the Miracle Range and made their first stop that night in the mountains. There, they met a contingent of Elves preparing for the invasion. Michael Desmond stopped the ship and descended to talk to their commander.

"We're set up in the pass, so they have to try to get through here," the commander explained as she gave them a tour through the snow. "We're setting up traps to destroy as many of the Zombies as possible. We have a laser squad, flame throwers, and grenades." Guns and such did little good against zombies, who had no working organs to damage. What was needed were weapons that completely disintegrated or dismembered an enemy.

"What if they send regular troops through to remove obstacles?" Asked Brendan.

"We hope we're prepared for it. We're concentrating on the zombies, because the troops don't want to be in front of them. That's a good way to get eaten."

They took off again, and Seamus Todd went to bed.

The next day, they were passing over the Balkans and they could see the enemy army.

"Oh, yuck," said Seamus Todd. He looked down on them through the telescope and saw every gruesome detail. The zombies were disgusting, and almost numberless. The Asuras must have gathered every corpse from the last age to build this massive army. The ghouls were in various states of decay, but they were coming in an endless wave. Finally, he went back to studying his books. The only way to stop the zombie apocalypse was the diplomatic way, and he was now a part of that effort. He'd often fantasied about beating the Zombies single handed with his strength and speed. That was foolish, he knew that now. No matter how much faster and stronger an Elf was than a zombie, their numbers would eventually overwhelm any resistance. But if they succeeded, the zombie army would be called back to the Regime, and they could go back to a watchful peace. In the meantime, he hit those books.

He learned quickly, memorizing one of Shakespeare's speeches into Neo-Persian. At dinner time, he recited it for Michael Desmond, Erin, and Brendan in English, Celtic, and Persian. He hoped they would like it, as well as seeing how well his lessons were coming along.

"Blow, wind, and crack your cheeks! Rage! Blow!
Your cataracts and hurricanoes, spout
Till you have drenched our steeples, drowned the cocks!
You sulfurous and thought-executing fires
Vaunt-couriers to oak cleaving thunderbolts,
Singe my white head! And thou, all shaking thunder,
smite flat the thick rotundity of the world!
Crack nature's mold, all germins spill at once
That make ingrateful man!"

Then a selection from the Rubaiyat of Omar Khayyam. The language had changed in the last five thousand years, but the message was the same.

Quatrain One Hundred and Four

"Yet ah, that spring should vanish with the rose!
That youth's sweet scented manuscript should close!
The nightingale that in the branches sang
Ah whence, and whither flown again, who knows?"

"That was wonderful," said Michael. "May I see you for a moment?"

He followed him into his office, wondering what he had done. He didn't think his bit of Irish brogue was too strong. It was more of a lilt, he thought.

"Are you gay?"

"Yes."

He had known since he was a child, he had always known. How had he given himself away?

"What's wrong with that?" He asked Michael.

"Nothing, by Elven standards. Where we're going, it can be very dangerous to admit it. So, keep it quiet. Don't let anyone know. Even diplomatic immunity might not keep you safe. These people are fanatical about it. And they're always looking for an excuse to kill someone."

"Good grief. So, we have to worry about Asuras with multiple heads and arms being prejudiced?"

"They don't consider alien heritage to be wrong, any more than we think being gay is wrong. It's a virtue, to them. They take pride in being descended from aliens. You should be careful."

"All right, I'll keep it under my hat." Though I don't see how, he thought. If you could figure it from just watching me, so can they.

"Thank you."

"I wanted you to get some idea of what we're dealing with." Michael drew out a book from his stack and opened it at random.

"What is this?" Seamus Todd asked. It was a mix of symbols. He recognized Russian and Greek, and thought some might be Sanskrit, but it made no sense.

Michael said, "This is what the Asuras saw when they examined our books. They thought we merely like looking at the shapes. So, one of their books is simply a collection of symbols, letters and numbers from different scripts."

"How can we deal with them when they're thinking is so different from ours?"

"That's what we have to work on."

It seemed they passed over the Regime army for days. There were even Elven zombies. A great black cloud moved over them, guarding them from the sun. Finally, they reached the main army. Here, he saw armies of Demons, Genies, and tanks gathered for a crushing assault on the west. They seemed to be expecting them, as they had a field cleared for the landing. It still wasn't large enough to accommodate the airship, but they sent the elevator tube to the surface and then used it.

They were met by a formal entourage and brought to the largest tent. Here, everything was fabric, gold illuminated by the light outside. They were brought before a couch that apparently served as a throne. Two servants with fans flanked the dais. Trumpets blared, and the leader of the army arrived.

Ravana was a young man of about twenty-six. He was the most two-faced man Seamus Todd had ever seen. Two identical faces grew from a single neck, and were joined at the ears. The faces were handsome, and there was some resemblance to Seamus Todd himself. It wasn't overwhelming, and they would never be mistaken for each other, but it was there. They had the same blue eyes and slender face. He wore a voluminous white robe, which made him seem bigger than he really was.

This was the first time he'd seen an Asura in real life. He'd seen them on the holo-vision before, but this was a new experience. Ravana's entourage of Demons surrounded him, and then one lone figure in a blue robe hurried in and joined the troupe.

He wasn't sure if he gasped. He may have. There stood the most beautiful guy he'd ever seen. He had raven black hair, light brown skin, and melting, slightly slanted eyes. Was this his dream man? He didn't look exactly like the blond-haired blue-eyed figure he always dreamed of. He was more handsome. His heart was thundering so loud, he thought everybody must hear it. He felt like every particle in his body was blown apart and put back together as something new. He had never believed in love at first sight before. He did now.

But as an Elf, he had to be careful. Not only because his sexual orientation might put him in danger. Elves mate for life, so they usually have long engagements to make sure two people were compatible.

"His royal highness, Prince Ravana," announced one of his entourage.

"Royal prince, it is an honor to meet you," said Michael, shaking him out of his reverie. He was supposed to be translating. He did so, quickly.

"Yes, I know," said the prince. "I am the heir apparent to the throne, son of prince Ratnavali, son of Emperor Harsha. This is my main councilor, Abdul Rashad," he indicated a somber looking Genie who had just spoken. The handsome boy waved. "And this is my half-wit illegitimate cousin, Rustem."

He felt an undiplomatic urge to throttle prince Ravana on his double neck. Rustem. His name is Rustem. Even his name is beautiful.

"We approach his royal majesty under a flag of peace, to meet the Emperor and plead for the release of the hostages," Michael Desmond said.

"This is an important matter," said Ravana. "It is very important your embassy comes through. I will accompany the ambassador to Babylon and speak for you before my grandfather."

"Your highness, this is too great an honor. I know we have our mission to complete, but so do you. Won't you get in trouble if you turn aside to help us now?"

"If you succeed, there will be no need for us to continue our mission. You heard me. We're going with them."

This was unexpected. The prince and his people were going to get on the airship and travel with them all the way to Babylon?

"We appreciate your offer, but don't know if we can accept it."

"I insist."

"Then I acquiesce. We will accept your embassy."

The Elves looked at each other and the Regime people looked at each other. Finally, they all trooped out. As Michael and a Genie came to the door together, the Genie said, "pardon me" in Persian, and Michael Desmond said "of course," in the same language. Then they started conversing fluently.

He knows Persian, he realized. Then what does he need me for?

Because it's expected, he realized. Translators are simply part of the entourage. Just like bodyguards. Even if they're not needed.

They entered the airship and they were off again.

Seamus Todd spread out his books on the glass floor so he could watch the world going on below him. He turned to "A Celtic-Persian Dictionary" and began doing his homework. He looked up. A shadow fell across his papers.

"Hi."

"Prince Rustem." He leaped up and bowed to the prince.

"You don't need to do that. What are you doing?"

"Studying Persian."

"I can help you with that."

"Can you? That would be great."

They spent two hours working on Persian. Seamus Todd was a fast learner and had used the language scanner, but there was so much to learn.

"Good," said Rustem finally. Why don't we take a break?"

They walked out into the observation deck.

"I knew I wasn't the only one," said Rustem.

"The only one who needed a break?" He stretched.

"No. The only one in the world."

"Like the quagga? There's more than one, now." Hunted to extinction long ago, the relatives of the zebra were now thriving once more.

"No. The only one like me."

"Oh." He looked into his dark brown eyes. Rustem's pupils were wide and dewy.

"Because there wouldn't have to be a law if I was the only one who ever felt this way."

They fell into each other's arms and their mouths met. Rustem's lips were like cherries, and they were just right, not too soft like a girl's, not too firm, just right.

They fell apart, gasping for breath.

"We have to be careful," Seamus Todd said.

"I don't care if we get caught."

"Well, I do. I don't want to lose you since I just found you. So, let's be careful, all right?"

"All right."

"Will you be in trouble if the Asuras catch you?" Asked Seamus Todd.

"Yes."

"Even though you're a prince."

"I'm nothing but an illegitimate son of the king," said Rustem.

"So, we'd be in trouble in your country?"

"Yeah."

"But not in my country."

"Yeah?"

"So, I'll take you home with me."

"Yes."

Seamus Todd said, "but until then, we have to be careful, all right?"

"All right."

"All right, I'll take you home when the mission is done. To the land of home and peanut butter apple pie."

"What's peanut butter apple pie?"

"You've never had one?"

"No," said Rustem.

They made their way to the galley, where the chef helped them find what they needed. In two hours, they had enough pie for thirty people, never suspecting it would be one person's last meal. There was enough canned fruit for ten peanut butter and apple, five plain apple, five cherry, five blueberry, and five pumpkins. They served them at dinner that night with whip cream, and Rustem said it was the best stuff he ever tasted.

Seamus Todd smiled.

After dinner, everyone trailed off to their respective cabins.

He hadn't been sleeping well since the attack on the lighthouse. After trying to force himself to rest, he tried studying. So he was awake when he heard a sound from the cabin next door.

His little room was up against Michael's suite. He strolled out in the corridor in his pajamas. Tiptoeing.

"Lord Desmond?" He ventured.

No sound. No reply.

"Michael?"

He continued down the hall and saw the window to the outside was partly open.

He tapped his watch. "Brendan?"

"Brendan here. What's wrong?"

"Hopefully nothing. I'm going to check with Michael."

"I'll be right there."

Seamus Todd decided not to wait. He climbed out the window. Sure enough, Michael's window was open, curtains moving faintly in the breeze.

The teenager made his way along the narrow ledge. He didn't call out. He no longer knew who might answer.

He crawled into the bedroom window, five hundred feet above the earth. Except for the light from the window, it was completely dark.

He scraped his foot against the edge. There was a flash of yellow, and someone was on him, his hands closing around his throat.

Seamus Todd fought back. Elves are slight but very strong. Males are almost all muscle. Being the youngest in a family of five had given him plenty of opportunity to learn defensive techniques.

Someone was pounding on the door. His consciousness was slipping away. He put all his force into a savage blow, and the grip went slack.

The door burst open. Brendan and Erin.

The figure behind him shoved him forward and jumped for the window. Seamus Todd started after him, but there was no need. There was a brief scream and the man in yellow slipped and Seamus Todd just had time to reach for him before he vanished in a headlong rush.

"Michael! Michael!' Erin was yelling, so he rushed back in as the light switched on.

Michael was lying in a pool of his own blood, which, like all Elf blood, was clear. His eyes were closed, and his skin was whiter than paper.

Erin opened a pouch and drew what looked like a red jewel to Michael's back. A vicious looking knife was pinned to his pinion, but it had prevented the blade from going further. The wound began to heal from the light of the jewel.

"He's lost a lot of blood. We have to get him to a hospital right away."

There was nothing to do but head west to a modern hospital in Italy, rather than going forward to the primitive conditions they might find in the Regime. Within an hour, they reached a city, and parked above the hospital parking lot.

They wheeled out Michael on a stretcher. Everyone came down the ramp in their night clothes, looking confused.

"All right," Brendan turned on them. "Who did this?"

"You don't think one of us did this, do you?" Asked Ravana.

"Well, he didn't do it himself. Who is missing?" Asked Brendan.

Seamus Todd, along with everyone else, was counting people. They were one short.

Finally, someone said, "Abdul Rashad."

"Where is Abdul Rashad?"

"How can we be worried about anything but Michael right now?" Seamus Todd shook his head and ran after the stretcher.

They had wheeled him into emergency surgery, and there was nothing to do but wait. Sadly, he returned to the zeppelin. When he got there, Brendan asked him to join him in his office. Erin was already there.

"I think we should cancel the mission," Brendan explained.

"But what about the hostages?" Asked Seamus Todd.

"It's very unlikely that the Regime will accept any one less than Michael Desmond for the position," said Erin.

"We have to try. Couldn't you do it, Erin?"

"They won't accept a woman."

"I'll work even harder on my learning Persian. Please. We have to do something."

"If we fail, the army can't fight back effectively," said the Elf Woman.

"And Tuatha will be invaded. It's unlikely we can defeat them, just because of their numbers," Brendan said.

"I think we should continue," said Seamus Todd.

Erin nodded her head. "I'm willing to try."

Brendan shrugged. "All right. But don't be too disappointed if it doesn't work out."

In the morning, he brought Michael a bouquet of flowers. Tulips. The sun outside was bright, but the hospital room was suitably dark. Michael was resting in the bed, his wings tucked behind him. As he got closer, the Angel opened his eyes. An old Elf like Michael was on his third life, and his wings were now feathered and broad like an eagle's.

"Good morning, McKenzie."

"Good morning, sir. I brought you these."

"How nice," said Michael.

"We decided to try to go ahead with the mission."

"I think that's a good decision."

"We can't do it nearly as well without you."

"Still, we have to try. When I get back to the dirigible, I'll give you a device you can put in your ear. We'll be able to communicate, and I can help you with your translations."

"That's great. I could use some help."

"And this." He indicated an almost transparent piece of plastic smaller than a contact lens. "It's a bug. Place this somewhere near the king's office and we'll be able to hear what he's planning."

"Thank you for trusting me, sir. I hope I can live up to it."

"Well, this is no time to retreat. Not if we don't absolutely have to."

That reminded him. "Michael?"

"Yes?"

"You said something about what you would have to do if worst came to worst, when you were talking with my grandmother."

"Oh, you heard that. Yes. It was to offer myself as a hostage, if nothing else could be done."

"So, it wasn't about killing them or something."

"Of course not, Seamus Todd. After all, we are Elves."

They were soon on their way again. Fortunately, they had been ahead of schedule. They would still be on time. They pushed to get from Italy to the Balkan Peninsula and toward Asia Minor. Soon, they were over the land again. And still over the enemy armies.

That night, he woke up, thinking he should check on Michael again. And felt someone was in the room with him. His hand reached out to catch the curtain, and the light revealed . . .

"Ravana." He had been transformed, like all Asuras at night. The face that looked forward still looked normal, but the other was all mouth with enormous teeth, as hideous as the most hideous demon.

"Surprised?"

"Disappointed."

"You killed my teacher," said Ravana.

"No, I didn't."

"He was told to kill Desmond. He failed because you killed him."

"He killed himself."

"Well, I am going to have to kill you."

"Why?" Seamus Todd retreated, trying to find an advantage.

"The yellow robes have never failed to kill a target. When one fails, the next in line is called upon to finish the job."

"So, you lower yourself to being a mere assassin?"

"I cared about my teacher, McKenzie. Like you care about yours."

"I care enough to die, not to kill for him."

"Strangely, that's just what the situation requires."

With a mental apology to the volume, he threw a book at him. The Bo Cuilagne. He knocked it aside.

"And there's nothing wrong with being an assassin," he sneered. "I've been trained by the best in the Regime. I am going to be a yellow robe."

"I've seen your country's covert techniques and frankly, I'm a little disappointed. You keep missing the target." He next tossed a package of tissues, but it wasn't enough to stop him.

Ravana slashed with his knife, but the chain holding his ring caught it and drew tight, deflecting it.

"Well, not this time."

The door slammed open, and Brendan was there. He seemed to fill the small cabin where the two young men were on opposite sides of the bed.

With a roar, Ravana sprang over the bed. Brendan caught him in midair. His dagger fell to the bed.

Erin looked in from behind Brendan's huge form as much as she was able. Meanwhile, Ravana's heads were flopping around as he tried to bite his captor. Brendan finally dragged him out of the hallway and pinned him to the wall.

"Let me go! Get out of my way."

"No."

"Why were you trying to kill McKenzie?" Erin began questioning him.

"Those were my orders. To kill the one who was protecting Michael Desmond. And then Michael himself."

"Why? He's just a boy."

Ravana sneered. "He's an Elf, isn't he?"

"You were under orders to attack us all?"

"Ask Abdul Rashad, when you get to hell. I thought I would start with the boy. It's my first assignment."

"Why lord Desmond? He's doing what you asked him to?"

"I don't know, I have my orders. Kill everyone who can get in my way, and then Michael. McKenzie. All of you. All I know is Uncle Pryadar didn't order it." He held out a hand with something tiny and yellow. "Let me go, now!"

Erin said, "you're not going anywhere."

"You won't be able to stop me," he said as he swallowed the pill.

"What was that?"

"Cyanide."

"Oh, no. You're not getting out of it that easily." She drew a white stone and held it to his flesh. At once the gem began to darken as it drew the poison.

There was a tapping on the wall from Michael's room. Seamus Todd rushed in to check him while the bodyguard and aide treated the two-faced man.

"What's going on," he whispered.

"Ravana just tried to kill me."

"Why?"

"So he could get to you. They're questioning him. He just took poison. He said I was protecting you, so they needed to get me out of the way."

"I see."

"I don't. Why are they doing this to us? He said Pryadar isn't the one who ordered it."

"He said that? I don't know. But you might have been the target at Brendan's, instead of me."

"Why?" Asked Seamus Todd.

41

"Because you're the king's grandson."

"I'll never be king." The Elves were basically one big royal family. He was far outside the line of succession.

"Royal blood matters to them. They want us all dead."

"Why are they trying to kill us?"

"Every form of life is sacred to them. Except human life."

"I have a hard time believing that."

"You might have to see it to understand it. Anyway, Ravana will be locked up. In the brig."

Early the next morning, as they were passing over the northwest part of the Regime, Seamus Todd decided to go see Rustem, if he could. Maybe they could talk. He wanted to figure out what he was doing in this whole mess before he discovered himself in over his head.

Rustem was being held in the same brig as Ravana. Though he was free to leave, he had chosen to stay with his cousin.

Just as he was approaching the guard to talk to him, they both heard the scream.

Oh, no, he was sure it was Rustem. He followed the guard into the brig, where a genie was crouched on Ravana's prone body. Rustem was trying to save his cousin, but his opponent was too large for him.

The guard opened the cell door and broke the attacker's grip. Rustem put his arms around Seamus Todd. He seemed close to tears.

"I woke up, and. . ." He made a throttling motion.

Though still horrified, he was also strangely relieved. It hadn't been Rustem getting hurt.

"He failed in his mission," said the Genie. "By our law, he must be put to death."

The guard handcuffed the assailant and knelt by the prostate form of the prince. His neck was bruised, with livid marks to show where his hands had been.

"This is bad," said the guard. He spoke into his watch. "We need medical aid right away. The prince is very badly hurt."

"With any luck, he is dead," said the rotund Genie.

"Quiet, you," barked the guard. He turned to the boys. "Are you all right?" He asked Rustem.

"Yes," he nodded. He looked shaken up.

Erin and another Elf, hopefully a doctor or something, came running in. They knelt by the prince.

"McKenzie, will you take Rustem out onto the promenade for a moment?"

"Sure."

The two boys waited outside for long minutes while they worked on Ravana. Finally, Erin came out. Her face told the story.

"I'm sorry, Rustem, we did everything we could. Ravana is dead."

"No," said Rustem. A tear slid down his cheek. "He had everything to live for. Why did he have to die?"

"Honey, I don't know." Erin took him in her arms. Seamus Todd joined them in what became a group hug.

"Shouldn't we take him to a hospital?" Said Seamus Todd.

"We will, but it doesn't look good."

They stopped at the next town. Ravana was wheeled out to a hospital, and his attacker was turned over to the local police.

The doctors only confirmed what they had known all along. There was no saving the prince who wanted to be an assassin. Ravana was dead.

Soon, they met in Michael Desmond's suite.

"You're not still thinking of continuing the mission after this, are you?" Asked Brendan.

"Well, we have to deliver the boys to their family, alive or dead. There's no one else to do the job if we don't," said Seamus Todd. He was glum, too, but he couldn't see the advantage of quitting.

Erin spoke up. "Those hostages might be in pain. They could be being tortured. I'd hate to turn around now, even though it seems the easiest thing to do."

Michael Desmond shifted in his hospital bed. He was recovering, but it would be another week before he could even get out of bed, and they were already past the northern border of the Regime. He had lost a lot of blood and was lucky he hadn't died.

"I know it requires a larger amount of service on your part than you might have imagined when you took the job. But we have to reach New Babylon anyway. Besides, his words when he thought he was dying indicate Pryadar is not behind the attacks. Someone else is. We need to find out who. If we fail, we fail, but I don't want to turn back at this late date. They would wonder why now, as I'm sure we're in range of their sensors."

"So, we go on and bring Rustem back to his family?" Said Seamus Todd.

"And his cousin, as well," said Erin.

"Well, since you are all so determined, I withdraw my objection," said Brendan. "I don't see we have any chance of success, but we will see it through to the end."

If nothing else, they had to drop off the body with the family. If they didn't, it would look like they were covering up his death. They also had to deliver Rustem, hopefully alive and in one piece. Seamus Todd understood that Ravana's father was dead, and the Ravana was next in line after Pryadar.

Ravana's mother of course was dead, as were most mothers of Asuras. Bringing children with multiple heads or limbs was hard enough in this world, and the women were of such little account as to be killed while giving birth was considered normal. Such a situation would never have been tolerated by the Elves, but to the Asuras it had become so routine they simply didn't care. A woman's life was never thought of as valuable as a man's.

CHAPTER THREE
The Changeling

The next day they reached Babylon.

They drifted over the suburbs until they came to the city proper. This was defined by a sloping black wall five-hundred-foot-tall, and wide enough to drive a four-lane highway on top.

From there, they could see their ultimate destination, though they were still some distance away. At their altitude the tower of Babel looked like a giant spike driven into the ground. As they drew closer, Seamus Todd thought more and more it resembled a huge figure, seated on a throne. The face of the carving was hidden behind a veil, a great headdress or nemes like the head of the Sphinx, surmounted the back of the head. Its outlines were clear enough. In one robed hand it held a globe, while the other rested on the armrest.

There was a plus shaped hole in its chest, into which the Globe slid comfortably. In fact, it seemed big enough to hold several ships of equal size. The four of them, Brendan, Erin, Seamus Todd and Rustem, came slowly down the landing pad. Only Rustem seemed excited to be home. The rest of them, even Seamus Todd, were gloomy.

A welcoming committee waited for them in front of a great gate thirty feet tall. Everything in this world, he reflected, seemed proportionately huge. There was no doubt it was impressive, though, to Elven sight, not especially attractive. Scale wasn't the only asset to architecture.

From here he could look out onto a portion of the city. Great clouds of black smoke seemed to rest over its demesnes, wrapping everything in gloom. Like the main tower, the city was a marvelous piece of work, but it was a city all of stone, metal and cement. If there were any trees here, he couldn't see them.

"Seamus Todd," Erin whispered, and he stopped staring into space and caught up with the others.

The leader of the welcoming entourage appeared to be a demon, with dreadfully yellow orange skin like a bright toadstool, wrinkled, over a skull like face. His skin contrasted with his black robes. His eyes were red and hard and mean like coals in a grate. Seamus Todd was as sure this was an enemy as if he had said so.

"Welcome to New Babylon," he lied. "We have been expecting you. I was told Prince Ravana was along as well?"

"We would like to see his uncle about that, first," said Erin.

"Of course," he said smoothly. "I am Duke Alexis, here to see to your every need. Please come with me."

They followed him into the cool interior of the castle. The heavy door shut behind them with an ominous sound, and Seamus Todd felt they were trapped. Except for Rustem, the others looked uneasy.

They wound their way through what seemed a labyrinth of tunnels and rooms, before coming into the main dining hall. A grand sweeping view met them, of a multi pillared room so vast they could barely see the other side. There were no windows.

The Asuras did not sit at tables and chairs like Elves but knelt at short tables or sat on cushions. The four of them and Duke Alexis were at the highest table, raised on a dais. Hundreds of other people were coming in and preparing to eat, and even more servants lined along the wall.

Seamus Todd looked at the utensils laid out for the feast. In addition to typical spoons, knives and forks, there was something like a pliers, something like a doorknob, and other tools of which he didn't have the least comprehension.

The food was spicy and not bad, though it wasn't as warm as he would have liked. Both at home and on the airship here, he was used to delicious food. He assumed the servants had to thread the seemingly endless corridors from the kitchen to the dining room. The food was served in courses, the first being a yellow soup.

"Eat up," said the Duke. "Surely you think our hospitality is good enough for you?"

"Of course," said the youth, and he reached for the soup.

It might have been delicious, warm. As it was, it wasn't too bad. It was a spicy, tangy soup. It might have been something like eggdrop.

Next followed a pasta dish, then a salad followed by the meat, then a sweet course. The desert was the best part, he thought, as it was supposed to be room temperature. It was something between a custard and a flan.

After dinner, they followed Alexis to another room. He realized the servants were expecting to eat what the guests had left.

"I will take you to lord Pryadar."

"Isn't he King Pryadar?"

"And many other titles. I'll get to all that in a minute."

They filed into the atrium.

"Presenting his majesty, King Pryadar of Mesopotamia, Pharaoh of Egypt, Duke of Asia Minor, governor of Afghanistan, regent of Western Russia, Emperor of Africa, and vice regent of India." Music played, search lights flashed, and a spot light glared. Very few people could live up to such an introduction.

This one could. A huge figure entered, seven foot tall. He had three identical heads, differing only in color. One was white as paste, one black as the night, one red as fire. He had too much long black curly hair, and long mustaches in the Indian style. His beards were black and with three points each. His jaws were long and saturnine. He had good features, but they didn't match. He wore a black and gold robe and cape with a breastplate of jewels over his six arms and two legs.

"Welcome to the Regime," he rumbled. All three heads spoke in unison.

"Lord Pryadar, we bring you greetings from the king and queen of Tuatha."

"Where is Michael Desmond?"

"My lord, he was severely injured and unable to come. I hoped. . ."

"I was promised Michael Desmond. You insult me by sending a lesser person. I said I would speak with Michael Desmond, and him alone."

Exactly as Brendan warned them. He tried to look like he wasn't thinking, I told you so.

Erin said, "your grace, no disrespect was intended. It was only because he couldn't come that he allowed me to take his place."

"No. Take your entourage and go."

"Your majesty, please." Said Seamus Todd. "Your nephew died."

"McKenzie, hush," Erin whispered.

"You have to know."

"What's this." There was a terrible silence. "My nephew?"

"I'm sorry, your majesty."

"You. You look a little like him, but you only have one head. I'll talk with you. Alone. Tell me what happened."

He followed Pryadar into his office. It was large enough, and a round, black marble desk dominated everything. He sat in a throne like chair and covered up the disassembled remains of a laser gun.

"An old hobby of mine, rebuilding ancient weapons." The boy leaned over the desk, attaching the listening device to the gun as he did so.

Seamus Todd told him about the treachery aboard the Globe, of the string of assassination attempts that left the prince dead. "His body is aboard the airship," he finished.

"I see."

"I'm really sorry, your majesty. I promise he didn't suffer much."

"Are you sure? To promise is to lie."

"I can only say I'm sorry, your highness."

"It's not your fault. I worried about him leading the troops and admiring the yellow robes. I never thought he would go so far."

"I think he was trying to impress you."

"It doesn't matter now. Well," he said abruptly, in a much lighter tone. "What about the hostages?"

"I think mourning your nephew is more important at the moment, don't you?" Though rescuing the hostages came was his priority, it seemed a diplomatic thing to say.

"We were close, closer than my own children. In our society, the uncle nephew relationship is normally considered the strongest bond. No, business first, then I will find time to weep later. You brought my brother's boy's body back, so that's one."

"One hostage, sir?"

"Yes. How many more can you free?"

"Well, we also brought your son back safely."

"Rustem? Good, at least you managed to return one of them," said Pryadar. "Anything else?"

"Well, I offer myself in exchange for the rest of the hostages."

"Ah, but see, if I wanted you, I could already have you," he pointed. "You're right here, after all."

Seamus Todd said, "oh, I don't think you'd take me without offering something in return. At least one."

"You make a throw and win. Very well, I will give you three hostages. And it's no good asking for any more at the moment."

Seamus Todd nodded. "Very well, I'll take three."

"You gave up too soon. You might have had four."

"Well, that's how things turn out, I guess. That's three more than we had before."

"Come with me and choose your hostages."

He followed Pryadar and his entourage into the elevator and they went up. Pryadar put his hand on his shoulder, and he wasn't sure whether to be comforted or creeped out. It was quite a way, and Seamus Todd might have thought they were must be in one of the highest floors, inside the massive head of the structure. Down another maze to the cells. These were covered with thick glass or plastic, a translucent haze in which he could see figures on the other side. Hands were pressed to the glass in response to his presence, hands all around.

"Wasn't there a married couple?"

"Yes. Release the couple. One more."

He closed his eyes, spun, and pointed. He chose a fairy, no bigger than his hand.

"Very good. That's three. They will be home by tomorrow night. I will have someone show you your accommodations."

"You mean, I'm not staying here with the rest?"

"I think you will be more comfortable in the rooms I've arranged for you."

"All right."

"Duke Alexis, show our guest his apartments." Lord Pryadar and the rest of his followers swept away. As soon as he was gone, the Duke's phony smile was replaced by a genuine scowl.

"What kind of name is Seamus?" Alexis snarled.

"It's the Celtic form of James. It means to supplant or trip up at the heels. What does Pryadar mean?"

"What do you think it means?"

"I don't know Hindu. If it was Celtic, I'd say it had the same root as Pryderi, which is "worry.""

Alexis replied, "I don't know what it means, supplanter. Ask him, if you get the chance. And you're here to supplant me, aren't you?"

"No."

"You may have fooled him, but you don't fool me. Give me your watch."

"My watch?" Asked Seamus Todd, horrified. His grandparents had given him the watch.

"You catch on fast. Give it to me. I know it's a phone and a computer as well."

He grabbed it and threw it to the floor, crushing it under his foot.

"And the listening device?" He held out a hand.

"No, don't give it to him," warned the voice of Michael Desmond in his ear.

Reluctantly, Seamus Todd dug the communicator out of his ear and gave it to the Duke.

"Now you don't have a way to contact your meddlesome friends. Good night," he sneered.

He was upset when he walked into the room, but it was pleasant enough. It had a window with a fantastic view of the city. There was a canopy bed, an attached bathroom on the right, and best of all, a library in one nook.

The boy figured he must be pointed west, because he could see the setting sun. He took out his Persian-Celtic dictionary and began working on it but was too tired to last. In a minute, he turned off the light and went to sleep.

In the morning, a servant opened the door. He garbled his name, but it sounded something like Humphrey, so Seamus Todd thought of him as Humphrey.

"Your trial starts in fifteen minutes."

"My what?" Seamus Todd started pulling on his pants. "My trial? I'm on trial? For what?"

"Your trial, your grace. You are expected in the royal court room in fourteen minutes and fifty-five seconds. Dress appropriately. Wear these."

Soon attired in a blue, green and white outfit, he was racing to keep up with Humphrey.

"Is this trial something to do with the hostages?"

"I believe it was your failure to kill the ambassador that they want to look into, Prince Ravana."

"You do realize I'm not Prince Ravana, don't you?"

"You agreed to take his place, so you are as good as Prince Ravana. You see, when someone is responsible for the loss of a life in our society, especially if it's by accident, the perpetrator's family is supposed to offer a substitute in his place. Sometime, not often, they might take two women for one man, but it's usually someone of similar age and sex," Humphrey explained.

"I'm an Elf."

"That doesn't matter. You'll do."

They entered the court room. Seamus Todd couldn't remember if he'd seen one before or not. There was a huge desk, the judge's bench, with a throne behind it, and purple curtains everywhere. Two tables, for the prosecution and defense, and a jury box. The rest of the huge room and balcony was filled with seats, which were beginning to fill.

Apparently, this was acceptable entertainment for the higher class. In the Regime, gladiator games were the main source of popular revelry for the hoi polloi, and courtroom dramas were for the elite. But the middle ground of things like theaters and movies were frowned on. (Though they occurred in clandestine spots and were popular among the lower classes and the young.)

"Sit here." He was shown to the defense table. A man with a cast on his arm looked up and smiled.

"What's going to happen to me?"

The man with his arm in a sling shrugged. None of his concern, Seamus Todd guessed.

He turned around and watched the audience. Most wore their finest clothes; long robes, gloves, hoods or turbans were in abundance. They also displayed their jewelry and finery for others to see. Hair colors never seen in nature were common here, as were faces covered in powder, rouge and make up. And that was just the men. The women were even more outrageously decorated. Their hats and headwear were obviously a contest of social rank to see who could wear the biggest and most distracting, since they were never allowed to go bareheaded in public. Some wore coins as jewelry, some were swathed in linen from head to toe. Soon a veritable pile of fur, wigs, gowns and paraphernalia threatened to overwhelm him. There wasn't an empty chair in the house.

He felt very much out of place.

"You?" A voice said. The walking sneer had arrived.

"They told me to sit here," he told Alexis.

"Leave him alone, Alexis," said Pryadar. "Don't make me warn you again." The boy was grateful for the intervention, but the Duke's glare could still have melted lead. The Prince and his entourage took their seats at the front, close enough to hear him when he turned around.

"I don't know what's going on."

"You see, you are bound by the code of honor of the yellow robes. You failed in your mission, so must pay the price," Pryadar explained.

"His mission was to kill me!"

"That will be dealt with in the trial."

"This isn't fair."

"This is an Asura court of law," said Alexis. "Who said anything about being fair?"

"It's a court of law. As good a place as any to discover the truth," Pryadar said.

The judge appeared from behind the curtain. Emperor Harsha. He limped slowly into his place, and his voice was like a raven's as he called the court to order. There was no need, because everyone had fallen silent.

Asuras are relatively long-lived, compared to Demons and Genies, though not nearly so long as long as Elves. Harsha was old even by Asura standards. He still seemed hale, though, if a bit shaky. It was obvious as he looked around that he was respected and even feared by the populace. He had been king for eighty years and had fathered two sons and seven daughters. As his illness progressed, Pryadar had taken over more and more functions of government, but he remained the supreme judge.

"I understand," he began, "my grandson is facing a heavy penalty for failure to kill a target as a yellow robe. Who speaks for Ravana?"

"Your honor, this young man and I do," said the man next to Seamus Todd. Unsure what to do, Seamus Todd merely nodded.

"And you are the prosecution?" He peered at the other table.

"Yes, your honor." A demon with a frilled headpiece like a triceratops and a saffron robe stood up.

"Do we have a witness?"

"Yes, your honor. Though we must not trust a single word he says, he must be considered a very unreliable witness. The prosecution calls Seamus McKenzie to the stand."

Seamus Todd felt all eyes on him as he stepped into the box lined with spikes. Many people were standing up to get a better look at him. Many had probably never seen many Elves in their lives.

The prosecutor shambled to the witness chair. "Young man, you were there when Ravana tried to kill the ambassador?"

"Don't I take an oath or something?"

"We know you will lie anyway," the prosecutor said.

"I'm not a liar," Seamus Todd felt his temper rising.

"Just answer the questions as they are asked. Where were you the night of Sagittarius the Ninth?"

"I heard a noise in my master's room and went to investigate. I discovered a yellow robe in his room, and Michael Desmond had been stabbed. When Brendan and Erin came in, the yellow robe jumped out the window and fell to his death. It was awful."

"Are you telling the truth?"

"I don't kid about food or assassins."

"And what happened with the prince the next night?" Asked the prosecutor.

"He came into my room and tried to kill me."

"How do you know what his intentions were?"

"He told me," said Seamus Todd.

"You consider the word of a murderer reliable?"

"I do when he says he's going to kill me."

"What else did he say, if he said anything at all?"

"He said when one yellow robe fails, another takes his place."

"Is that what he said, word for word?"

"Ravana said, the yellow robes have never failed to kill a target. When one fails, the next in line is called upon to finish the job." Then he said Pryadar hadn't ordered the assassination. Did you ask for the recording from the Globe? I'm sure they have it."

"We're not interested in doctored tapes," said the prosecutor.

"The tapes wouldn't be doctored. They're more reliable than eyewitness testimony."

"Who told you that?"

"You did."

"You think you're smart, don't you?"

"No."

"You think you're smarter than me."

I think most varieties of eggplant are smarter than you. "No," was all the boy said.

"Prince Ravana came into your room and tried to kill you."

"Yes."

The Prosecutor sneered, "What if I said you tried to kill Michael Desmond?"

"I'd say you're nuts."

"You had the motive, means, and the opportunity."

Seamus Todd said, "none of the above. I don't have a motive for trying to kill him."

"You wanted his job, I'll wager. That is reason enough."

"For you, maybe. No Elf has murdered another Elf in five thousand years."

"There's a first time for everything."

"Not this, there isn't," Seamus Todd tried to keep from losing his temper.

"I think you tried to kill Michael Desmond and blame it on an innocent man."

"Do you have any idea how much his getting hurt messed up our plans? I was just supposed to be a translator. Then I found myself thrust into the middle, and because of that I ended up here. Why on earth would I do that?"

"You didn't know you would be caught. Murderers always think they won't get caught."

"I loved him."

"Love," sneered the prosecutor. "A handy title to pin our crimes to. Crimes are committed in the name of love all the time."

"Only if they don't understand it."

"Do you know something about love I don't?"

"I think I do, if you say it leads to murder."

He pointed at Seamus Todd dramatically and shouted, "you would have killed him, aren't I right? If you can prove your innocence, do so."

"It's not my job to show I'm innocent. It's your job to show I'm guilty. The knife I saw in his side came from the Regime."

"Did you save it?"

"No, the hospital kept it after it was removed."

"Convenient."

"I didn't do it. Abdul Rashad did it," Seamus Todd said.

"And how convenient he is not here to testify."

"He's dead. Someone could testify for me, though. Brendan Penrod, Erin Macomber and Michael Desmond."

"They are not here. Michael Desmond isn't here."

"I should be allowed to call them to testify, then," Seamus Todd said, wondering where his friends were.

"They can't testify, they were not called as witnesses."

"Then the trial should be postponed until everyone is here."

The prosecutor said, "that would cause a delay in justice being done."

"No, it wouldn't. It's the only way to get justice."

"We are used to justice being delivered swiftly, however it is done among the Elves."

"It's done right," Seamus Todd quipped.

"Are you showing contempt for this court?"

"It would be hard to show anything else."

"Impertinence!" Shouted the prosecutor. "I would like this witness to be held in contempt until he learns to answer my questions."

Harsha leaned forward. "I think he's doing an excellent job, considering the nature of your questions." Suddenly, Seamus Todd liked the old judge better.

"Your honor," he said.

"Yes?"

"Am I being tried for trying to kill Michael Desmond or failing to kill Michael Desmond?"

The prosecutor said, "Prince Ravana. . ."

"I am not Prince Ravana."

"You are now, so pay attention."

"I am not Ravana."

"Then where is he?"

"He died," Seamus Todd said.

"While in Elvish custody."

"At the hands of one of his lieutenants."

"According to Asura law, the Elves owe us another life in recompense."

"Well, I'm here to do that. I'm a changeling. But I'm not Ravana himself and I never would be, even if I tried, so why bother?"

"Because it's your duty."

"I can replace him. I can't become him."

"May I say something?" Said Pryadar.

"Your majesty."

"I realize that no one can replace my nephew. Still, what the Elf is doing is noble and honorable. I will accept him as a substitute."

"That's very high minded of you, your majesty. You, young Elf," the judge peered at him over his glasses. "You must answer the questions as if you were really Ravana. He knows you're not, so just do your best. Please answer his questions."

"Thank you, your honor."

"Did you kill Michael Desmond?"

"Why would I kill him?"

"To get his job."

"It didn't work that way. Erin was the one who ended up with his job," Seamus Todd explained.

"And yet you say she didn't want it."

"I didn't say that. She was unsure she could fill such big shoes, and that the Regime might not accept a woman as an ambassador."

"So, you took the first opportunity to slide yourself into his position."

"I put myself forward because I felt bad for him. I told Pryadar about his nephew. I figured he had the right to know."

"And you ended up filling Desmond's shoes."

"That wasn't my intention."

The Prosecutor. "A lot of things didn't go by your intention, did they."

"No, like the assassination attempt."

"But it played into your hands."

Seamus Todd said, "nothing went right, that's how I ended up here."

"The fact is, there have been four attempts on Michael Desmond's life, and you were present at all of them."

"To prevent them."

"Is that your job?"

Seamus Todd said, "only by chance."

"Michael had bodyguards, didn't he?"

"Yes, but we weren't expecting any trouble."

"So, you weren't prepared for an attack on his life?"

"No." He didn't add that they should have been more prepared after taking the Regime retinue on board.

"I believe I have heard enough."

"Your honor," protested the Prosecutor. "We've barely begun."

"He's answered your questions. Since he is taking Ravana's place, he can only be tried for royal crimes, and murder doesn't count. No prince of the royal blood can be punished except for the three crimes of royalty. Treason, sedition, and homosexuality, the crime that we do not speak of."

That's a punishable offense, even among royals? Seamus Todd thought. And murder isn't?

There was a flurry of activity in the court room as someone burst through the door and ran down the aisle. It was a girl about his own age, maybe a year older. She had curly hair, but her tresses were gold and in small ringlets. She wore one large ring in her left nostril and was dressed in pale gold.

"Who's that?" Seamus Todd whispered to the man in the sling who sat next to him.

"Pryadar's daughter, Grand Duchess Naganandini, heiress presumptive."

"Your honor, your honor, may I examine the witness?"

"Yes, you may."

The court room, which had been silent, became a buzz of whispers as she strode past the tables on the way to the witness box.

"Do you know who I am?"

"I'm lucky to still know who I am."

"I am Naganandini, princess of the Regime. Prince Ravana was my cousin."

"I'm sorry."

"Well, don't be. You've made me heiress presumptive of the realm."

"Don't you even care about your cousin?"

"Why would I do that?"

"Because he was part of your family."

"So?"

"So, I'm supposed to be doing what Ravana would do. They're asking me to take his place, and I'm doing my best. But I'm no Ravana."

"I knew the prince. I agree, you're no Prince Ravana."

"Thank you."

"What do you mean by that?"

"I mean, the only reason Ravana didn't kill somebody is he had bad aim."

"Liar. My cousin was trained by the best assassins of all time. There is no way he could fail unless he was sabotaged by someone else."

"I caught him sneaking into my quarters."

"Or he caught you sneaking around Michael Desmond's quarters."

"If I was going to kill someone, I could have done it before we left Tuatha." In fact, all he would have had to do was nothing, and let one of the attempts succeed.

"Then you wouldn't have had anyone to pin it on, would you."

"Elves don't kill each other," he said simply.

"But Asuras do, are you saying that?"

"Asuras kill each other. And Elves."

"And Elves kill Asuras, is that right?" Said princess Naganandini.

"Historically, it has happened."

"Are you saying it's all right?"

"I'm saying because of the Perpetual War, there has been a lot of useless killing on both sides. But if we would just stop the war, the Elves will leave you alone."

"Why do you say Elves don't kill each other?"

"Because it doesn't happen." Seamus Todd pulled on his collar nervously.

"So, if a murder occurs, blame the nasty Asuras, is that it?"

"If a murder occurs, follow the evidence to the truth."

"Do you know the truth?"

"I know I didn't do it."

"Enough," said Harsha, starting. "Since the Prince is of royal blood, another must take his punishment."

"His cousin, Rustem, would do," said Alexis.

"No, not Rustem. He didn't do anything," Seamus Todd was on his feet. He found himself hating Alexis more than usual.

"Rustem will return to the head of the army, where he will lead the attack on Tuatha," said Pryadar.

Well, maybe that wouldn't be too bad. Though it left him hoping the attack would fail but Rustem would survive.

"Your majesty," purred Alexis, "weren't you going to make an announcement about the succession while the entire court is gathered here?"

Harsha nodded and removed his robe, revealing his imperial military outfit beneath. "Well, we will see. Which of my heirs loves me the most, will inherit the kingdom. Pryadar, my only living son, you go first."

"Sire, I am the enemy of all other loves than yours. Consider the graciousness you've shown me in my education, being your son, and my loyalty to our kingdom. I not only am prepared for the kingship, I deserve it. For you I would abandon my wife, my children, everything I own, the kingdom, even life itself. That is how much I love you."

"Well said, my lord. You have assured your place in the succession. Now, Naganandini, say your part."

"Granddaddy-waddy, you know how much I love you. More than anyone or anything, I need no kingdom, but only to enjoy our time together. My heart and soul belong to you. I love you more than I can say, except that it is more than anyone or anything. I ask only to be by your side."

"Splendid, granddaughter. I am glad my love means more to you than any kingdom, because you're not getting one."

Her face changed from cheery to fury.

"You promised me my fair share if I said I loved you. Now give me my share!"

"You were content with my presence, but I must send you to Tuatha to replace the Elf."

"I deserve my share of the kingdom. Let me have it!" She was almost crying, not with sorrow but with rage. "I hate you!"

"Enough. And lord Ravana, what do you say?"

Seamus Todd cleared his throat. He said, "your majesty, this whole thing is wrong. I can't speak for the dead, but I can speak for me. You've seen how competition for the throne only sets people apart. Stop this. My people have a story about something like this. In King Lear. . ."

"See, you crows, how the Elf refuses to flatter me. He speaks the truth, while you were out only for yourselves."

"Your majesty. . ."

"He is the only one who deserves to be king," said Harsha.

"Please, stop. You don't have that kind of power, to change the succession," said Seamus Todd. Sure, he would love to be king, who wouldn't, but he was sure it would be very dangerous to defy Pryadar and Naganandini. Asura politics could be extremely nasty. It would be very different from being king of Tuatha. That would be all right.

"I can do anything I want," dribbled the Emperor.

Seamus Todd said, "not if it breaks the law."

"I am the law. Your plainness has won me over. There is no need to say more."

"Don't be flattered by lack of flattery."

"Do you love me, yes or no?"

"Not enough information. I don't even know you. We met twenty minutes ago. Give your love to your granddaughter. She wants it."

"She doesn't deserve it."

"Then neither do you."

There was a communal gasp from everyone else in the courtroom. Seamus Todd stood, quietly defiant.

"Again, he speaks the truth. Pryadar remains heir presumptive, and lord Ravana will follow him in the succession. As for Princess Naganandini," he stopped in time to see her. She swept up the small clock on the table and threw it at the Emperor. It missed, hitting the curtain behind him.

"As for Naganandini, she can only be heiress if something happens to Prince Ravana."

"That is enough," Pryadar told her sternly. He turned to the guards. "Take her from the court room."

They took her by both arms and removed her, gently but firmly. Red faced, she fought them all the way out the doors. "I will be queen; do you hear me? It's my right! I'll show you, I'll show you all."

"Be silent," said Pryadar.

"You, I'll kill you, I swear I will. Do you hear me, father? You're dead."

Still resisting, she was dragged out into the hallway.

"Now that that's over," said Harsha, "I'm sending her to the Elf kingdom as a hostage, in exchange for the Elf we have. And I want the matter of the hostages cleared as quickly as possible."

Pryadar agreed. "I will leave the details up to you, but I agree. It must be handled expeditiously. Court is dismissed."

The Demons and Genies and Asuras all filed out, leaving Seamus Todd and Rustem alone for the moment.

"We're to be separated," said Rustem.

"We'll get back together."

"I hope so."

The guards looked at them. It was time to part. They surrounded Rustem and marched him away. Seamus Todd was alone in the middle of Babylon.

Threes

The number three is the chosen number of the Elves. There are three types of Elves in Tuatha, Island or Celtic Elves, Scandinavian Elves, and Continental Elves. From the beginning there were three strains of Elves, as well. Sprites, which are the tallest and most human, Gnomes, which are about three feet tall, and Pixies, which are the smallest, about one hand high. Each in turn can transform into another being, like caterpillars into butterflies. Sprites can become Angels or Giants, Gnomes can become Dwarves or Sylphs, and Pixies into Fairies or Brownies. Each has a special skill as well, inherited from the animals which were crossed with human DNA to produce them.

Pixies – flight
Fairies – hypnotizing
Brownies – healing
Gnomes – transmute earth
Dwarves – Speak to animals
Sylphs – control plant growth
Sprites – stunning
Giants (male) Warp Spasm
       (female) sonic scream
Angels – flight

CHAPTER FOUR
The Wedding of Aliyah

Life became routine around the palace. In the mornings, he would get up and work on his languages. He never knew if he would be needed, or for what purpose, so he tried to shower and dress early, in case they called for him. Breakfast was usually brought to him and slid through the slot. Lunch and dinner were in the communal dining room.

Two days after the trial, Humphrey came for him again. "Training," was all he said.

He followed him through the maze to a class room. Other boys his age were already there. And one girl. The teacher was an old Genie with a long black beard, and a patched orange robe.

"Today we will be working on fencing. Everyone, pair up and practice. Prince Ravana, you may do as you like for the next three hours."

"Is this assassin school?" Seamus Todd began to understand why Ravana had failed as an assassin while being convinced he was one.

"I don't want to be an assassin, I want to learn," he said.

"Your uncle would be most displeased if something were to happen to you."

"Nothing will happen to me, I'll take it easy, and how many times do I have to say it, I am not Ravana."

"Princess Aliyah, will you practice with the prince?"

"It will be my pleasure," said the girl. She was as pretty as Naganandini, maybe prettier, but she seemed nicer. She had cinnamon hair, bright blue eyes and a pleasant smile of bright white teeth.

They faced one another. Swords drawn.

"I'll take it easy on you," he promised.

"Don't even think about it, pretty boy," she said with a smile.

She made an obvious strike. He countered, striking her sword to the side.

"So you're not completely hopeless, after all. But let us see how you do if I stop holding back."

She was good, but she was no match for him. Like all Elves, he was very fast. In a moment, he had her disarmed and a sword to her neck.

"Strike, then and quickly," she challenged him. "Finish it."

"I'm not going to hurt you." He dropped the rapier and turned away.

Suddenly she had his sword and was slashing at him with all her strength. He dodged nimbly to the side. In the next second, he was up behind her with his hand locked on hers, raising the sword and forcing her to drop it.

The teacher was watching them and tottered over. "You would make a sorry assassin," his teacher said. "You turned your back on an enemy."

"You're right, I would. Why don't we try repairing engines or something useful?" Said Seamus Todd.

"Continue the training."

They continued for the better part of an hour. Then the teacher had them draw up in a single line and take on Seamus Todd one by one.

He might have done better if he weren't so tired. As it was, the sixth person in line managed to take him down. Then all of them jumped him. He was at the bottom of a pile of people, struggling to get free. The teacher shouted, and they broke off. Seamus Todd managed to sit up, gasping for air.

The teacher seemed grudgingly impressed. "Yes, you are quick. You might have what it takes after all."

"Thank you."

They worked on throwing and catching knives, then focused on disguises for an hour. Costumes were fun. It was too bad it all had to be in preparation to commit crimes.

That evening, after dinner, the Emperor summoned him.

He followed the Emperor out to the very top of the Tower of Babel, in a dazzlingly beautiful sunset. There was a railing around the edge, but it was to give a desperate faller a last chance, not to give them a place to stand.

"I brought you out here, my favorite view, because for once I wanted to share it with somebody who wasn't going to try to push me off."

Now that he brought it up, he could push him off. The old fool deserved death many times over. He let the moment pass.

"I brought Pryadar here and showed him the kingdom. He tried to overthrow me. Literally."

"How old was he then, lord?"

"Fourteen."

The same age Seamus Todd was now. "I'm sure it didn't mean anything at the time."

"I think I have made a grave mistake. Pryadar will be the ruin of my kingdom. I cannot choose between my country and my son."

"I'm sure if he had actually wanted to kill you, he would have." The boy didn't know if that was much comfort.

"Like most Asura Emperors, I had many wives. Two sons. My younger son died in an accident. Now, my grandson is dead as well."

Seamus Todd wondered about Pryadar and had the feeling it hadn't been only an accident. He didn't mention it. All he said was, "I'm sorry, your majesty."

"What's done is done."

"Well, you still have one son and two grand kids. You managed to give your kingdom that."

"I'm concerned for Pryadar. I know my reign is drawing to an end. The doctors gave me a year, no more. Maybe less. Maybe considerably less," Harsha looked off into the distance.

"Your majesty. . ."

"You will keep an eye on him, won't you?"

"Of course, I will."

"Then I will sleep better."

After a moment the Emperor resumed speaking.

"Pryadar was supposed to have at least two male heirs to the throne, but he only had one girl, and the other is illegitimate. Since Naganandini is the only living descendant, it is possible she may take the throne someday. Unless someone else inherits it." He looked at the youth meaningfully.

"Your majesty, I'm an outsider, I'm not Asura, I'm an Elf."

"You are of royal blood, and that is all that matters. You are acceptable in a way no Demon or Genie could be."

"Look, everyone dreams about ruling the world. I know I do. But Asura politics have a way of turning nasty, and I'm not sure I'm prepared."

"We will prepare you."

"Naganandini is. . ."

Harsha interrupted. "Insane? Probably not technically, but with some severe personality problems."

"I was about to say the rightful heir. Wouldn't you feel better if she was made queen? I'm not fond of her, but it's because, like you said, she has problems, not because she's a girl."

"The people will never accept a woman."

"They may, if you say it's all right. Stand up for her, declare her next in line, and the people will go along with it."

Harsha said, "I'm afraid you overestimate them."

"Then what does that say about my ability to be king?"

"I want you to at least consider it. The list of Asuras is small, and you are more acceptable than any other candidate. There's me, Pryadar, Naganandini, and Rustem."

Seamus Todd sighed. "All right, I won't say no, either. But I won't be too disappointed if it doesn't turn out."

"You have to hope it turns out, because there's only success or failure before you. Rivals for the throne are not dealt with lightly."

"That's what I thought. Thank you."

The Emperor explained a little about their history. "When the war between the humans and the Poids ended, our people settled in three cities, all along the equator. We do prefer heat. Our ancestors settled in India, where we were almost worshiped as gods. We do have some noticeable similarities to their myths, so we called ourselves Asuras. Then, many years ago, when I was just a boy, my father came here and conquered the Middle East. He was a very strong man, but he regretted his conquest cost so many lives. He was haunted by it forever after.

"When I became king, I decided to consolidate what we already had instead of conquering other nations. I thought I did well."

"You did," Seamus Todd said.

"To focus on the welfare of my people instead. But all I have done is in danger of being undone. Pryadar moves to make war, and I cannot do anything to stop him. Maybe you can."

"If you couldn't persuade him, your majesty, I don't see how I could. But I'll try," Seamus Todd said.

"Thank you."

Time passed as he lived in the palace. It would have been easy to complain, but he tried not to. His days were spent mastering the Persian language, and he was now proficient in it enough to read books.

He was disappointed in the first book he read in Persian. Its subject was Elven books and movies that portrayed Asuras in an unfair light. Sometimes, Seamus Todd thought the author had a point. Asuras did appear as villains in books, plays, and films. The author seemed to vent his worst wrath on things like "The Vancouver Incident," or the "Weehawken," events that actually happened. They were historically accurate, and if his people didn't like being labeled terrorists, maybe they shouldn't indulge in terrorism. At the end, its message was not a plea for greater tolerance, fairness, and diversity, as the Elves would have if they had written it, but a jihad against the Elves. That would teach them to make charges against the Asuras. There was being sensitive to fairness, and then there was being too easily offended. Admittedly, he complimented balanced portraits, which the Elves usually tried to produce. There were also many stories, based on the Arabian Nights and other tales, which featured people of Genie culture as the good guys. There were relatively few good Asuras. But then, there were few Asura actors. He finished the book and hoped the next one would be better.

He was trying to learn more about the culture he was in. His next book explained Asura history. From this, he learned there were only a handful of Asuras at any one time. The genes that passed on were very volatile and not infrequently fatal. And since Ravana's death at present there were only three full blooded Asuras; Harsha, Pryadar, and Naganandini. Women were exceedingly rare among Asuras. Fewer still lived to old age. Pregnancy was often fatal to them. Pryadar's current wife was part Genie, part Demon, and was only his consort. She could not rule in her own right. Crossings of Asuras with Asuras was always sterile or fatal. Demons, on the other hand, were fairly common. While Asuras were the descendants of humans infected with the virus, Demons were the results of animals, humans, and the virus.

The virus began on another planet, guiding the development of the dominant life form, the Poids. The Poids in turn had come to Earth in their spaceships to start the conquest. The humans and Elves had resisted fiercely, and ten years of war had almost destroyed all three races. The people of Earth were too strong to defeat, but they couldn't drive the aliens from the planet. The Poids were unable to continue their attack with the supply lines being millions of miles and millions of years away. Finally, the Poids admitted defeat and left for home. The virus that infected them, though, had already spread to earthly life forms. There, it began to multiply rapidly, creating the Demons and the Asuras. War began between the Elves and the Asuras, but again it ended in a stalemate. The humans were unable to compete, leaving behind several daughter races. The Elves settled in the northern regions with its temperate climate, while the Asuras and their allies settled the equator. Besides the Elves, who were created as a result of scientific experiments, there were seven human races. There were the Kachina of North America, the Amazonians of South America, the Genies of West Asia and the Middle East, the Ethiopians of Africa, the Easterners of East Asia, the Southerners of Australia, and the original humans, who supposedly still lived on islands scattered across the Pacific.

The Asuras, in turn, had conquered the Genies and much of Africa and Asia, to create the Regime. In trying to duplicate the long lives of the Elves, they used the original viruses, but only created the Zombies. Not alive but animated by viruses into a grotesque parody of life, they were the Regime's terrifying strike force. Not the least bit clever or even strong, they overwhelmed their enemies by sheer numbers. Seamus Todd realized if they were going to win, they were going to have to defeat the virus itself. The zombies were vulnerable to sunlight, but great clouds hid the marching army, and there was little hope of lifting the gloom.

A knock on his door. Who was it but Naganandini?

She came in and put her hand on his arm and nudged him toward the bed.

"I want you to sleep with me."

"No."

"You are the captive. It's an honor to make love to you."

"No."

"Why not?"

"You're not a nice person, Naganandini."

"I'm trying to give you a chance."

"No, thank you."

"You must be gay."

"Yes, I am."

"You freak."

"See. You're a princess, a grand duchess, but you're so full of hate. . ."

"I could tell everyone, you know."

"Like you said, I'm the captive. I don't think they're going to care."

"You have no idea what you're dealing with." She stormed off.

The Loved One

is an honored captive among the Asuras. Naganandini would not have been the only female to offer to make love to one, as this was the custom. The captive (who was always male) was well treated and given every luxury, but he could be killed if the treaty was dishonored. Any attempt to escape was looked upon as treaty breaking, but few ever tried to escape.

The next day, he was at lunch when someone shouted across the room. He knew who it was.

"You. You queer."

He turned to see Princess Naganandini bearing down on him.

"Me?"

"You humiliated me in front of everybody!"

He realized she was talking about the court room scene the other day. "You did a pretty good job all on your own."

She raised her hand to slap him. She surprised him, but not nearly as much as he surprised himself. He caught her wrist.

"No."

"I challenge you to a duel!"

"A duel? Are you crazy?"

"Never call me crazy!" She struggled to pull free. Finally, he let her go.

77

"No."

"You have to, or you'll be called a coward."

"I can live with that. Better than having to fight a girl."

"Fight me, queer. You're going to fight me. The arena games are tomorrow. I'll see you there."

He didn't want to go, but when Humphrey showed up at his door, he realized he wasn't going to be able to get out of it.

"I'll be serving as your squire, sir," he said brightly.

He and Humphrey went into the armory. The wall was lined with swords, lances, clubs, tridents, guns, lasers, shields, and every other weapon imaginable.

"What's this?" He indicated a glove with sharp spikes attached.

"A gauntlet."

"Can it be used for disarming an enemy without hurting them?"

"Yes."

"I'll take this, then."

"You're allowed a shield with that."

He chose a silver one with a green butterfly. The butterfly was the emblem of his house, and representative of the Elves along with the Celtic cross and stone dogs, were their emblems, it seemed appropriate.

He entered the arena, the largest room in the entire obelisk. People filled the stadium. Except for the Emperor's box, they all seemed to be standing, so perhaps it didn't have chairs, or they were only brought in for longer occasions. He hoped this would be short.

Naganandini appeared at the other end, to the cheers of the crowd. She was dressed partly in armor, including a high Roman helmet, an upper armor of plate metal, and a red dress. Lugging along a mace longer than she was.

"What's the red dress for?"

"In case I get your blood on me."

"Shake hands and come out fighting," said the Emperor.

Seamus Todd raised his left hand to shake, and barely missed the first lunge.

"And she's not even going to shake hands," said the announcer blandly. "We're just going to go right into it."

He raised the shield to block the next blow and was knocked back but still standing. The morning star probably weighed as much as she did. It was almost pathetic.

"Princess, we don't have to," swing, "do this."

"Let your weapon do the talking, Elf boy."

"This isn't getting us anywhere."

"It's getting you one step closer to hell!" Her lovely face was contorted into something horrifying.

She circled him halfway around the arena, trying to use brute strength to match his speed. Seamus Todd remained on the defensive, tiring her out.

Naganandini lunged again with the mace, and this time he didn't just take it on the shield, he grabbed the weapon. Now he was doubly armed, and she had only her shield.

"Your highness, this is enough. I'm not going to hurt you. . ."

"You already killed me, so I'm just returning the favor."

He examined the mace, summoned all his strength, and swung it against the wall. It broke in two, and he picked up the handle.

"Maybe you'll manage it better now, your highness."

Her only response was to leap at the morning star and try to drag it out of the dust. She managed to hoist it shoulder high and ran at him.

Back and forth they dueled in the sand pit. As she got more tired and red, he continued to push her, wearing her out. Time after time she lunged and he dodged, like the cobra and the mongoose. He was the mongoose, he realized, and must use the furry little animal's weapons. Speed, persistence, against sudden strike and venom. Eventually, he would tire her out.

"Can't we discuss this. . ."

"Over your dead body." She screamed a war cry and charged him.

"Did you order the attack on Michael?"

"I don't need assassins to kill him, any more than I need someone else to kill you."

He stepped out of the way, and she swung again.

He circled round, looking for an opening. He found one and seized her by the crested helm.

"Let me go!"

"No."

"Let me go!"

"Do you surrender?"

"I'll kill you for touching me."

She leaned all her weight away from him, and he let her fall. She landed on her bottom, and was up in a moment, redder than ever.

"Give up yet?"

"I'll kill you." She rushed him so fast he was surprised at her agility, but not as surprised as he was at his own. He spun around and was behind her while she was still heading where he was. He shot out the gauntlet hand and caught her by the shoulder.

She spun around in rage, and again, he moved behind her. She swung the steel mace, twice, and the second time he let her go and caught it instead. When he leaped away, he had the mace.

"You're disarmed, Duchess. Why don't you surrender now?"

Her only answer was a snarl of hate so extreme even he was taken aback. Unarmed, she rushed him as if she would tear

80

him to pieces with her bare hands, but he easily bounced away. With the heavy shield and mace, she was now faster than he was. All he could do was outlast her.

She managed to grab the shield as if she would wrench it and his arm off together. He let her claw at it desperately, until he saw one of her fingernails was bleeding. Distracted by pity, he lowered the shield.

She tore straight for his eyes. He snapped the shield up, blocking her, and felt a solid impact as the rim caught her in the chin.

She fell backwards on her heels, stunned.

"Are you all right?"

"I'm going to kill you for this," she said, as she sank to the dirt.

"It seems we have a winner. Seamus Todd McKenzie."

Most cheered him, some booed. It had been a lively exchange.

One person who didn't cheer was a demon in the first row. "May I challenge him, your Majesty?"

"Get in there," said Pryadar.

The demon was gigantic, the head of a boar, orange-red, with four arms on a massive body that looked like it had been sculpted from mashed potatoes. He wore a small loincloth.

"What happens if I surrender?"

"You die."

"That's what I thought." He took off the gauntlet and threw it at the Demon's feet.

"What trickery is this?"

"Just getting ready."

The gigantic demon struck first, and Seamus Todd sidestepped it. Before he could recover, Seamus reached out and touched him. He knew he would have to hold longer than an average sized person. Still, the Elven touch worked.

The Demon looked around, confused, then came crashing to the ground.

"And he nails him with a stunning touch for the victory. Way to go, Elf!"

The applause was thunderous, but it would have been the same if he had lost.

Pryadar clapped his hands. "That's enough. Prepare to go to Tuatha, Naganandini."

"I hate you."

He tried to help her up. "Get away from me," she snarled.

"Finish him off," commanded Alexis. He meant the other demon lying prone in the sand.

Seamus Todd's response was to walk out of the arena.

"Folks, he seems to be forfeiting his victory."

"Get back here and finish him." The crowd was split. Some applauded him, others wanted to see somebody die. A mix of cheers and jeers followed him out of the lists.

Later, they called him to say goodbye to Naganandini. She was carrying a suitcase, and dressed in the long, flowing Elven style. One by one she said her goodbyes.

"Grandfather, I hate you."

"Father, someday I'm going to have power. Someday, you'll kneel before me and beg me for your life. And I won't give it."

"Well, you just try, sweetheart," he replied.

Next was Duke Alexis. "You're the only one who accepted me for who I am. I won't forget that when I come into my kingdom. You were my only friend."

Finally, Seamus Todd. "I hate you most of all."

"I tried to be kind."

"Save your pity. You're going to need it." Snoot in the air, she stormed off and boarded the air vessel that would take her to Caer Wydr, the Elvish capital, set in the Danish Peninsula.

The night Naganandini left, he and the Emperor ended up discussing literature.

"One of the oldest stories in the west is about a beautiful princess kidnapped to a foreign city," Seamus Todd said.

"We have that story too. We call it the Ramayana."

"We call it the Iliad."

"I read that one. In the original Greek."

Seamus Todd said, "our story is the Bo Cuilagne, the Cooley Cattle Raid. It's older than the Elves and has been rewritten and told many times. It was written in the Fourth Age, so it's more than six thousand years old."

The Emperor said, "Our story is the Shah Nameh, the Book of Kings. It was written in the fourth millennium of the Fourth Age, so it's about the same age."

"Cuchulain is the servant of a king. He defends the Brown Bull of Connaght from Queen Maeve and her entire army all by himself."

"Rustem is the champion of a king." His chest puffed out with pride. "He defends Persia single handed from the armies of Demons."

"Cuchulain accidentally kills his son," said Seamus Todd. "I never liked that part."

"So did Rustem."

"Cuchulain was slain by treachery at the end of the story."

"So was Rustem," said Harsha.

"Maybe we're not so far apart as we think."

"Maybe there is common ground."

"But it's the way a hero's story is told that makes it individual. It takes a lot of care to draw up individuals instead of types. Now, in King Lear. . ."

"My favorite," said the old king.

"You've read Lear? Has it been translated into Persian?"

"I read it in the original English. I can read English, though it's been so long since I've spoken it I can't really remember."

They stayed up for hours, discussing books.

"Are you growing older, sir?" Seamus Todd tried to be polite.

"It's my night form," he explained. He wasn't greatly changed, but he looked more wrinkled and decrepit than before.

"You change at night?"

"All Asuras do," explained the Emperor. "Don't Elves change?"

"Some do," Seamus Todd said. "Not all of us do. Some of us are shape shifters. Those who can, can change into anything, but they tend to pick one animal shape and stay with it. It's complicated."

"Can you, lad?"

"No, I'm too young. But I hope to be able to do it someday."

"Good. Show me when you can." They finally went to bed.

Several mornings later, there was a knock on the door. Humphrey again.

"Congratulations, sir. We must get you ready for the wedding."

"Who's getting married."

"You are."

"I'm getting married. I'm fourteen. Elves seldom get married before -to who?" As he followed him down the hall.

"To Princess Aliyah, of course. Do you have any other fiancée'?"

"We call it betrothed."

"It's all one, my lord. Here are the royal fitting rooms." He pushed him inside. "Good luck."

Two women came forward to dress him in a blue suit. They even painted his face in blue swirls. He covered his antenna so they wouldn't get covered as well.

"It's a good thing my eyes are blue, or I suppose I'd have to wear contacts."

"How did you know?"

He couldn't tell if she was serious or not.

A knock at the door. A surprise visitor.

"Erin!" He was relieved to see her again.

"I'm so glad you're safe. I am here representing Tuatha and Michael Desmond."

"How is he?"

"Much better. He got out of bed yesterday but wasn't up to a wedding yet."

"Good. That he's doing better, I mean."

"We talked to your mother and told her everything that happened. I'll call her again and tell her what is going on after the wedding."

The chapel was a green dome. He couldn't be sure, but he thought they were in the globe in one hand of the figure. They marched him down the aisle. everyone in the congregation on his side wore blue, too. Even here, many were trying to outdo one another in outrageous clothing, so long as it was blue. The other side of the aisle, the bride's side, was all in red.

Aliyah appeared at the back row of pews and swept forward as the music swelled. She was dressed in red, a good color for her, but so bright that it looked more like a prom dress than a wedding dress. Her veil and train must have taken miles of lace. Her skin was decorated in henna.

"If you kiss me, I'm going to bite you," she whispered furiously.

"This wasn't my idea, either."

"It wasn't?"

"No. I'm sorry we have to get married, but since you lost your betrothed, it was the least I can do."

"Well, thank you."

"Dearly beloved, we are gathered to celebrate the wedding of Prince Ravana the Fourth of the Golden Land to Princess Aliyah of Persia. Do you take this woman to be your lawfully wedded wife, to have and to hold, in sickness and in health, until death do you part?"

"Go on," she whispered. "I don't mean a word of it, either."

"I do," he lied. Suddenly, she wasn't the only one who was red. Under the paint, he was blushing from his forehead to his neck.

"And do you, Princess Aliyah, take Prince Ravana for you husband, to obey, as long as you both shall live?"

"I do." She didn't blush, or even hesitate. Well, having grown up in the palace, she was probably used to lying.

There was a great deal more, but that was the essence of it. The people of the Regime liked their ceremonies long. As it was, morning was gone and afternoon was wearing on, when they finally finished. Then came the reception.

This took place in the main dining room, now festooned with golden curtains, red flowers and blue balloons, overdone like a wedding cake. It was hideous.

Seamus Todd was starving. Eagerly, he awaited dinner, but all that was served was cake and punch. In an Elf wedding, which he had been to, dinner was always part of the festivities. He had been looking forward to a steak or chicken or something nourishing. He was really hungry, so he bit into the cake eagerly. It was too sweet. Sickeningly so. He gulped it down as best he could.

Then came the dancing. He danced first with Aliyah. She was a pretty good dancer, too, but Seamus Todd was among the best in a country of dancers. The onlookers watched appreciatively as he sailed around the room with her in his arms.

Then he danced with Pryadar's wife, Queen Hagar Semiramis of Babylon. She reminded him of a toad, with warts and staring eyes and a dozen chins. She was almost unbelievably ugly, but she had a kind smile, and let him lead her out on the dance floor. Then Aliyah's mother, and so on down the line. He even danced with some of the men, including Pryadar, and apparently this was all right. He didn't understand sometimes how their minds worked. At the end of their turn, Pryadar merely said "you dance well," and he was gone.

One of the guests he ended up dancing with was humanoid, but definitely not human. He resembled a rough statue of a man, covered in moss.

"I am Thirididar. I am the last Poid left on Earth," he explained.

"I thought your people left five thousand years ago."

"Most of us did. There was a small remnant left behind to finish what we had started."

"You mean the conquest of our planet? Isn't that pretty hopeless by now?"

"It's not over yet. We Poids don't live as long as Elves, but we have long life spans. We may see you conquered yet."

Then came Erin. "My prince, you dance divinely," she teased him.

"Thank you. My parents started teaching me when I was very young."

"Congratulations. This should mean you can move more freely around the castle and the kingdom."

"Aliyah and I don't get along that well."

"That's an act. You can trust Aliyah with your life."

"Why? Are you saying she's a . . ."?

"Hush." She whirled him around the dance floor.

So, Aliyah was a spy for the commonwealth? How far could he trust her? Spies, by definition, were untrustworthy. Their mission was more important than human lives. Could he help out by gathering information as well? If he was expected to spy for them, was he to report to Aliyah?

She had one more warning for him. "Whatever you do, don't go to Pryadar at night, when he takes his true shape. No one may see his face and live."

"I'll remember that."

"I mean it. If he wants to meet at night, run out into the desert alone, you'll be better off."

"All right, but I don't think he's really a bad guy."

"Be careful, he has a heart of gold. Made of metal."

They had to switch partners just then, so he only caught a glimpse of her face as they pulled away from each other.

The evening wore on. Seamus Todd hoped more dinner would be coming, but there was only the vile cake. The sweet punch, however, was replaced by champagne, as the festival continued.

He took a glass as it was offered to him and tried a taste. He wasn't averse to wine, especially at his own wedding, but he didn't like it. Apparently, it wasn't real champagne, but a cheap wine passing itself off as being from the finest vineyards of Tuatha.

The toasts began. Harsha led them off, mumbling "to such and such on such a such glad such and such."

Everyone applauded, so the speech must have been a success. Pryadar was next, and his toast was articulate, though he ran on a bit.

Duke Alexis was further down the line, and said "to the young couple," as if he was wishing the plague on them.

The toasts ran on, congratulating her for a lucky match. Aliyah blushed.

As evening fell, Pryadar and most of his entourage disappeared before he could change. Alexis stayed for some reason. The Queen, though, apparently had no trouble transforming in front of others. He felt the warmth of flesh melting in front of him, and she turned into a toad like monster, with bulging eyes and green flesh covered in warts. The Demons also shifted into their true forms. The wedding party turned ugly.

He turned to Aliyah.

"Well, congratulations." It was all he could think to say.

"For what? Being married against my will?"

"So, is this what's it's like here? You're allowed to say anything as long as it's yes?"

"This is what it's like. Women are chattel. There's nothing we can do about it."

"I'm going to do something about it right now."

"Oh, no. Don't." He was already stumbling to his feet.

"I have something to say."

People were turning towards him.

"Excuse me, I have something to say."

"To Aliyah, who takes being married against her will with such grace."

"Not here and now, you fool." Aliyah pulled on his arm.

"You people are selfish, dancing on this young woman's dreams. Shame on you. You offer her up like a sacrifice, without a thought about how she feels about it."

Aliyah said, "I'm sorry, folks. Ignore him."

"Don't apologize for me. I am not drunk, I had one sip. I'm mad. I think you are cruel to demand this girl to be married when neither of us wanted it. Is this Asura hospitality? Is this Asura honor?"

"You've seen our hospitality in that you still draw breath," said Alexis. His arms were crossed but he was smiling as if pleased at something.

"Exactly. It's really not hospitality at all. Nor is it honor, to force people to marry against their will."

"Pay him no mind," said Aliyah. "He's just confused."

"You use people for your own ends. You don't care about who they are or what they need. You gamble with lives like poker chips. Well, it's not right."

Alexis said, "that's enough. You question our very way of life." Of all those who had transformed, the Duke was the most horrifying. He looked like a skinned corpse.

"That's what I mean to do. Question all this? Why can't a woman make her own decision about who she marries?"

"Next, you'll be questioning why we hate Elves."

"That's a very good question. Why do you hate Elves? We've never done anything to you."

Aliyah was hiding in her veil with her hands over her face. "Because you exist."

"That's not good enough. That's what I think." He sat down.

"He's only saying what he thinks," said Harsha at last. "No harm will come to the Elf for speaking his mind."

"He insults our hospitality," said Alexis.

"Enough, I said."

Seamus Todd got up and left. Nobody stopped him.

He returned to his room, washed off the blue dye and sat on the edge of the bed. He hadn't acted like the diplomat everyone said he should be. He had blown it. And he knew it.

Elven Society

    is structured somewhat like social insects. A fertile king and queen have numerous offspring, which are in turn fertile. For example, Caroline, daughter of Blake and Margaret was a fertile female who married Sean McKenzie and they had five children together. Their children would also be fertile, but the further one gets from the original pair, the more likely they are to be sterile. After several generations, most Elves are sterile. The fertile offspring mate with commoners and thus the line is continued.

    Despite this, Elves have a strong belief in equality, and the king and queen are only firsts among equals. New kings and queens are elected from the pool of available candidates, and usually, a couple where one is the son or daughter of the previous rulers that already has children, has the inside track. The current heir is Jason Aldoreth of Caer Wydr.

CHAPTER FIVE

Translated

Next morning, a visitor. Aliyah. She opened his door and came in. "I think what you did yesterday was very brave. Thank you."

"I made a mess of everything."

"You spoke the truth. They don't like hearing the truth."

"I want to go home."

"So do I. To my own people," said Aliyah.

"Even though they traded you off for this?"

"You were traded by your people, too."

"I had a choice in the matter. You didn't. We can help each other escape."

"Are you kidding?"

"I don't kid about food or escaping," said Seamus Todd.

"When I am free, I can decide where to go. Perhaps to my family in Persia, or perhaps to the Genie settlement in Cologne. It's up to me, isn't it?"

"Can you get a letter I write out of here?"

"It's risky, but I think so."

"Good."

He wrote it out and gave it to her.

"How will this help us escape?" Asked Aliyah.

"It won't, I just wanted to get a letter to my folks. Are you serious about wanting to escape?"

"Yes, I want out of here," said Aliyah.

"Then I'll take you with me."

"Do you promise?"

"To promise is to lie," Seamus Todd quoted Pryadar. "We'll do it. We'll find a way."

"What is life like among the Elves?"

"It's difficult to describe. Elves aren't like Asuras or Demons."

"That's a good thing."

Seamus Todd said, "well, for one thing, we get to choose our own mates. Elves mate for life, so we have to be very careful who we pick."

"Do they beat their wives?"

"Do they what?" Seamus Todd's mouth dropped open.

"Do they. . ."

"I heard you. I just never heard of such a thing. Do husbands beat their wives here?"

"It happens."

"No Elf woman would stand for that. Or her family. Yes, things are very different there."

"Tell me what your life is like so I can compare it to mine."

Seamus Todd was born at Caer Wydr, the capital, on Aquarius First, 5511. Like most Elves, his childhood had been a happy one. There was the castle to explore, thousands of books to read, people to see. He would dash through the palace on his imaginary steed, pretending to be a prince and knight in shining armor.

When he was eleven, things changed. The war started again, and Mom insisted on moving them away from the palace and its wonders. He had been happy there. They moved to the lighthouse that summer. Mom was on a self-reliance kick. They were going to grow their own food in their own garden. And she promised to keep a light on in the tower until the war ended.

First his father, then his older brother, Thomas, were called into the service, and Christian volunteered. He wanted to go, too, but Caroline was firm. Her youngest son was going to stay safely on the farm.

Things didn't go quite as she planned. Siobhan and Shannon didn't like being taken from the luxury of the glass castle to a little village on the edge of nowhere. Seamus Todd ended up doing most of the gardening, fishing and other chores. It also fell to him to fix all the broken stuff, because he was the only one left in the family with any mechanical inclination.

So it was until the night the Demon and his Genies had come to the lighthouse, and his adventure had begun.

"Do you want to go back to the castle?"

"More than anything."

"That's why you want the war to end?"

"That's one reason."

They talked for a while, discussing ways to escape. They didn't come up with any one plan but agreed they would find a way.

Thirty hours until he meets Pryadar at night.

Several days later, they came for him to go on a military expedition. He wasn't sure if this was meant to be a punishment or not. They traveled to the southern end of the Arabian Peninsula. He met Pryadar and Alexis in their tent headquarters.

There was a large computer-generated map on a table. Pryadar showed him the battle plan with a computer simulation.

"We're leaving a gap where the enemy might escape. What are these soldiers doing here?"

"Why, those are your honor guard, prince Ravana."

"How about we move them over here, to prevent the enemy from escaping." Then he wondered what he was doing. He was for the rebels, wasn't he? All he knew was, he knew how to lay out a battle plan. The time to show mercy was after you defeated them, not during the battle.

"You would dare reemploy the men whose job it is to protect your life. I never heard. . ."

"Be quiet, Alexis. The boy is right. We don't have a large force in the south and every unit counts."

"My lord. . ."

"Enough."

Seamus Todd waited in his tent as he heard the guns going off. He watched from the safety of the tent, then paced. He could see the lasers as they shot through the dust storms raised by galloping hooves and heavy mechanical feet. The beautiful war song of the native people rose and fell, and finally fell silent. The rebels were brave, but their cavalry and guns were no matter for the six-legged Morgoth tanks, air power and lasers. Periodically, a staff member brought him updates. Finally, the rebels were defeated, and the surviving leaders rounded up and brought before him. The line of prisoners wound out of the tent and seemed to go on forever.

They had only to look at him to tremble in fear and fall on their knees before him.

"Lord prince, have mercy."

"We fought only because we were poor."

"Well, what did you think I was going to do to you? Go back to your homes and start taking care of your fields. Take your horses, as you'll need them for planting. May the Emperor bless you. Go on and have good lives."

"Thank you, your majesty," there was much bowing and kneeling and weeping, as they left the tent.

Eighteen Hours

After awhile, Alexis came storming in. "Where are the prisoners?"

"I let them go."

"Tell me you didn't."

"None of them were bad people. They simply wanted food. So I told them to go back home and grow it. They're simple farmers, after all. . ."

"You idiot! I was going to put all those men to death for their rebellion! They, and their followers and their families, were all under sentence of death!"

"Then I'm glad they were sent to me first."

"I grow tired of your arrogance. The Emperor seems positively taken with you, and Pryadar may be fond of you, but I know who and what you are. You will never be an Asura."

"Thank you for the compliment."

"This will come back on you. You will live to regret it."

"Are you threatening me?" Asked Seamus Todd.

"I'm endangering you."

"Get out of my tent. You're just jealous. They like me, and I'm not even sure you know what love is."

"I don't because it doesn't exist." Alexis was almost shouting.

"You'll make a serious mistake if you underestimate love."

"This will come back on you, I promise."

"Get out."

"I know what you are. And the prince will know it soon."

"Go ahead." Said Seamus Todd.

Four Hours

The next day, Pryadar knocked on his apartment door. Seamus Todd thought Alexis had made good on his threat, but the Asura didn't even mention it. "I wondered if you would like to take a day and see the city."

"I sure would, your grace."

"Get dressed and meet me at the gate. It will just be the two of us."

It was the two of them, out on the town. It was hard to disguise a seven foot, three headed Asura and an Elf, but it didn't matter much. They were recognized anyway. They hadn't gone very far when an old woman threw herself at Pryadar's feet.

"My lord, have mercy."

"Why, whatever is the trouble, my dear?"

"My son is accused of a crime he didn't commit."

"Tell me what happened."

"He was arrested for a crime he didn't commit. His is a death sentence. Please, lord, put forth your hand and save him."

"Then they will find him innocent."

Sure, right, thought Seamus Todd.

"His execution is tomorrow. Please, my lord."

He raised her out of the dust and patted her hand. "There, there, dear. There is nothing more to fear. I will have your son pardoned at once and returned to you. Safe and unharmed. I will send a message to the court as soon as I get back to the tower."

"Thank you, my lord, thank you," she bowed as she backed away. "I will never forget your kindness."

He must know the case pretty well, if he knows who to pardon, thought Seamus Todd. Maybe he's not such a bad guy after all. Maybe he really does have a good heart.

They came to a second citizen, a Genie with a long black beard. "Help me, lord. Grant me succor, succor, I beg you."

"Succor," said Pryadar. "But make known to me what you need done, and I swear I will grant it. Speak now, don't be afraid."

"My family is desperately poor. My wife is sick, my son is in the army, and I fear I will have to sell my beloved daughter as a slave."

"Enough, my good man. Take this. I am sure it will be enough to pay your debts and more." He brought out a sack of money he must have just happened to have on hand.

"Bless you, your Majesty. Bless you," he kissed Pryadar's ring and departed.

"On to the bazaar."

What a market place it was. The strange music of the Genies was heard everywhere, like the music of falling rain on leaves. Vendors mixed with acrobats, mimes, sword-swallowers, magicians, doomsayers, ragged urchins, and women of the evening, contending with shoppers in a milling crowd.

"It's really something," Seamus Todd said, not wanting to be impolite. The Elves were much more decorous, but to each his own. The smell of fresh fruit and vegetables mixed with spiced meat, fish and perfume until it was nearly overpowering.

Two hours

They had a late lunch or early dinner at a nice Genie restaurant. Buttered chicken with curry, and banana fosters for desert. It was nice to have a hot meal, and one away from the palace. The food was delicious, especially without the sand that seemed to get into everything in the casbah.

Over diner, Pryadar explained. "Our people have an ancient custom. If we have shared food together, neither can harm the other. We are bonded."

"Our people have the same belief," Seamus Todd replied. "I'm glad we share the same custom."

"Are we bonded?"

"We're bonded."

"So do you trust me?"

Seamus Todd froze. He'd been warned several times, by several different people with different motives and observations, not to trust this person. He'd begun to relax and see his good side, but now it brought a sharp stab of suspicion.

"Don't you trust me?" Pryadar asked.

But he was on a diplomatic mission. He couldn't offend the person he'd traveled thousands of miles to see.

"Yes, I trust you." It wasn't true, but it seemed the right thing to say.

Forty minutes

They passed a street vendor selling cotton candy. Ha hadn't had any since he moved to Ireland, and Pryadar bought him a cone.

"You were warned about me, weren't you?"

"Your majesty?"

"Not to trust me."

"It came up," he said reluctantly.

"Not everyone understands what it is like to be the most powerful man on earth. Not less but more than the average citizen, I have to obey the law. I have to do what is best for my kingdom in the long run. It's not an easy burden. Perhaps you can understand that better than most."

"I can, your majesty."

"I was born with a heart condition. Left untreated, I would already be dead. Instead, I had an artificial heart installed. A heart made partly of gold."

"Oh, so that's what they meant when they said you had a heart of gold."

"Yes," said Pryadar. "But I like to believe I'm a better person, for having suffered like other people. It humanizes me, don't you think?"

"Yes, my lord."

"So you trust me."

"I trust you," said the Elf.

He threw the last of the cotton candy away. He felt sick at having to lie and yet still strive to trust the enemy. Why did things have to be like this?

"Good. I think I've thought of a way to set you and all the other hostages free."

"You have? That's wonderful."

"Everybody wants something from me," Pryadar sounded like he felt sorry for himself. "Even you."

"Well, you're the most powerful person on the planet," Seamus Todd said. "You hold all the cards. If you would let the hostages go, people might see you for the wise and generous person you are, not just a. . ."

"Yes?"

"Someone who would hold Elves hostage," he finished.

"We'll fix that," he said. "Let's go home."

"Which home."

"Mine. We'll see about sending you to your home."

They were halfway back when another stranger approached them.

"Halt, prince."

"Who dares to speak to me in such a manner?"

It was an old man in a long robe. His clothes were tattered, but the man and his beard were immaculate. A soothsayer, obviously.

"Pryadar, I know what you are planning to do and you must not do it."

"You stay away from this boy." He pushed himself between the old man and Seamus Todd. "You don't lay a hand on him, do you hear?"

They hurried away. "Sorry about that, lad. There are weird people in this city. Were you afraid?"

"No," he answered truthfully. He thought the old man merely odd, but he had repeated the warning he had already heard.

"There are those who would enjoy hurting children. I'm sorry you had to see that. Now, why don't you go wash your hands and meet me on the eighth floor below ground in say, ten minutes?"

"Seamus Todd looked at the setting sun. "*Get away anywhere you can, the desert, whatever you have to do. Don't meet Pryadar after dark.*" His sense of duty strove with his fear.

"Yes, I'll be right there."

Ten Minutes

He ran back to his room, changed his clothes, and hurried back to the elevator. He got off on the eighth floor underground and stepped into a vestibule. There was a single white door in a white wall.

Touching it, he felt a chill, but he was underground, after all. The entire building was probably cooled by the underground extension.

He opened the door.

And reeled backward, scrambling over himself, choking, gagging, afraid he would throw up. He ran for the elevator and pushed the button eight times at least.

Bones. The whole room was lined with bones, and he was pretty sure they hadn't been cattle. An ossuary.

The elevator was coming down slowly. Why didn't it hurry? He pushed the button several more times.

"No, no, no, no, no, no, no, no, no." He staggered back and tried to run, when he heard the elevator door opening at last.

He expected to see Pryadar, but it revealed Duke Alexis and two guards.

He backed up to the wall, with them closing in on him.

"Don't use your stunning ability. Just come along, nice and easy."

"Please, no."

They dragged him into the torture chamber. The walls were covered with yellowing human bones, artistically arranged; rows of thigh bones, piles of pelvises, and a chandelier made of vertebrae. Alexis turned on one guttering candle and ordered him chained to a chair.

"Now, boy, I have some questions for you."

Seamus Todd's eyes were squeezed shut. "No, no, no," was all he could muster.

"Open your eyes, boy, or they will be opened for you."

Somewhere far away, the curfew bell hung. Alexis smiled. His flesh began to melt. Seamus Todd could feel the heat from his transformation. When it was over he looked more than ever like the walking dead – a fleshless corpse, all bones and muscle.

He raised a hand with a scalpel in it. "Did you think you were the hero of time? I am offended by that attitude. Now, let's begin."

"You sent the assassins after Michael and me, didn't you?"

"Yes. Now I'll ask the questions."

"What do you want to know?"

"Why is three the number of Elves?"

"That's what you want to know?" He could have asked for that at any time and gotten an answer. Seamus Todd dared to hope he might survive. Maybe this was just a game, though a nasty one. "I don't know, it just always has been. There are three types of Elves, Fairies, Gnomes and Sprites. When they transform, they can be one of three more, making three times three, nine. There's the sun, moon, and the stars, three sources of light. There are three jewels in the crown, diamond, emerald, and sapphire, for love, truth and honor. The number for the Easterners is five, and the Kachina, four. I don't know why. My favorite number is eleven." It was the most neglected number. "Also. . ."

"I don't think that was a good enough answer." He held his hand to the boy's face.

"What are you doing?"

He made numerous small cuts on his face, in the shape of a Celtic cross. It took all his will to not scream as it cut into his skin.

"Why is green the color of the Elves?" Alexis demanded.

"Green is the color of new life, of plants and trees. Most Elves look good in it. I don't know." His favorite color was cobalt blue.

He couldn't believe this was happening to him. "Please could I have a rag?" The sting was excruciating, and only a forewarning of what was to come.

"Be patient. What is the substance of the Elves."

Oh, good, he knew this one. And besides, they were mixing with the blood on his face. "Tears. And we cry not only for ourselves but for all the pain in the world. If you are in pain, the Elves will help you. . ."

Again, the blade flicked and this time he screamed. Alexis cut off the tip of his right ear. And ate it.

"Stop that. Quit your crying. Now, to business. Each time I cut you and you don't scream, I will set a hostage free. Do you understand?"

Seamus Todd said nothing, didn't even nod his head, too afraid to move or respond. *It hurts – it feels thick as a thumb and dull as a spoon, I'm bleeding, it hurts –*

He did better than most, but he was an Elf, with greater focus of will. It took all he had. Five cuts. Five freed prisoners.

On the sixth one, a groan escaped his lips.

"That was five. You made a sound."

"But I didn't really scream."

"I say you did. Let's continue."

"Seven cuts. You did it, boy. Now, they're free."

"Can I go now," he whimpered. *It hurts –*

"Not so fast."

One of the guards spoke up. "This is enough, my lord. He's just a boy."

"Who are you to tell me enough, slave?"

"If I am a slave, I do you service by telling you enough."

"How dare you."

The guard's only reply was to draw his sword.

"Don't just stand there. Kill him," Alexis said to the other guard. He started to draw his sword, but the heroic guard was on him and felled him in a moment. He then turned on Alexis, who by that time had snatched up a heavy hammer and managed to brain the guard who had tried to save the boy.

"No," Seamus Todd was shaking and sweating, and tears were running into the blood on his face.

"Now, where were we. Are you a worshiper of the darkness? Admit your people are the worshipers of darkness and our people are right, the people of light, and your torment will end."

"But we're not. We're people of the balance, both yin and yang, darkness and light. Each is born of the other, and there can't be one without the other." Seamus Todd's voice trembled.

"I warned you."

"You're not of the light."

"But I am. And your recalcitrance provokes me. We are the people of light, superior to any other. You are one of the sons of darkness, from the west where the sun sets. You are a worshiper of night!" Alexis slammed the table with his fist.

"No, I'm not."

"What do you worship, then?"

"Nothing."

"You don't worship anything?"

"No." He revered his ancestors, he loved nature, but he had never found anything in this world, including himself, that was worthy of worship. Worship, he believed, was in fact, sin.

"Very well." Alexis selected another scalpel. "I believe you should worship lord Pryadar."

"No."

"You're not in a very good position to say no to me."

"I don't care. I don't worship Pryadar," said Seamus Todd.

"Say, I love Pryadar."

"I love Pryadar."

"I worship Pryadar."

"No." The Elf said through gritted teeth.

"Say you worship Pryadar."

"No, I won't." Seamus Todd almost shouted.

"You think I can't make you say anything I want?"

"I will not worship a false god. Pryadar might want to be one, but he's not. And I won't worship him."

"Yes, you will, my prince. I can make you say anything I want."

"No, you can't."

Seamus Todd was perhaps in less pain than an average human would be in the same situation. Elves are tough, almost impossible to dominate.

"Mom, Dad, Thomas, Christian, Siobhan, Shannon, Doug, Rustem, Grandpa, Grandma. . ."

"Do you think reciting their names will help you? Now, is the world round?"

"Well, of course it's round. Even you know that. The Poids would never have found our planet if they were still thinking the world was flat," Seamus Todd said.

"That wasn't what I asked. Do you think the world is round?"

"Yes." Said Seamus Todd.

"Yes, the world is round." He slashed at him again.

"Please, stop, please!"

Alexis asked next, "why is the Celtic cross the symbol of the Elves?"

"I don't know," Seamus Todd sobbed. "It's been the symbol of the Elves for thousands of years, so why not keep it? It's very different from the horned skull sign which is the sign of the Asuras."

"Now for the real question. Are you gay?"

"Yes," said the boy.

"Did you know Rustem was one?"

"Yes. Are you one?"

"How dare you?" Said Alexis.

"Pretty easily. Why does it matter to you?"

"Because I am opposed to this evil you call good. Don't attempt to lump me with your evil. I am nothing like you."

"Look me in the face and say that." The tears and blood were running down his face like melting wax.

"It is my handiwork. It's an improvement. Now see if anyone will ever love you."

"Please don't do this to me. When Pryadar finds out. . ."

"When Pryadar finds out." Alexis mocked him. "He ordered this treatment for you, Shameless Toad."

"You're lying."

Alexis sneered, "I don't have to lie. That pathetic old man is behind me. What are you doing?"

"Please, stop. Father, mother, Thomas, Christopher, Siobhan, Shannon, Rustem. . ." He was shaking and pale. He was going into shock.

As he reeled in and out of consciousness, he thought he saw the door open, and a monstrous shadow filled it. It was a giant spider-like creature with three heads, many eyes and arms, black and brown. It walked upright. He was reminded of Shelob in Lord of the Rings "a tower of hide and horn," but worse. The figure carried a sword.

"My lord Pryadar, what are you doing here?"

Instead of answering, he stabbed the Duke through the stomach. He fell back, driving the sword partly into the floor. Pryadar stomped on him in his heavy boots.

Pryadar started slashing indiscriminately at the corpse, over and over again.

One moment, he was there with his face a mass of cuts and blood gushing over him – and the next, Seamus Todd was suddenly free from pain.

It was over. He felt his body falling forward, and he wasn't part of it any more.

"Cardiac arrest," gasped Pryadar. As the boy's body fell to the floor. He put his lips to his bleeding mouth and tried to restore his breath.

"No, you can't hurt me anymore," he thought. "My worst fear came true, and it's over. It's over, and I'm free."

Seamus Todd lifted his hands and accepted the darkness waiting to overtake him.

Pryadar the monstrous spider swept the boy into his arms. "Sorry," he muttered.

There's no need to be sorry, the boy thought as thought escaped him. The worst has happened, and it is over. They couldn't break my spirit. My body, though, has to go.

It was too late. Seamus Todd had bled to death.

The monarch turned and carried him up the elevator.

CHAPTER FIVE
Part Two

Meanwhile, back at the lighthouse, they had received Seamus Todd's letter.

Dear Mom and everyone,

I am doing fine, and how are you? I traded myself to Pryadar and got three hostages freed. I'm still working on the rest.

Michael Desmond got hurt on the way here, so we have had to improvise as we go along. Erin ended up leading the embassy, but they wouldn't take her because they'd been promised Michael. This whole place is kind of messed up.

I like my room, it even has a library. Here's a picture of it. (Please see photo.) I can look out on the city of Babylon and pretend I can see all the way to Ireland.

I should write dad as well and tell him how I'm doing, but I'm not sure where his unit is. Perhaps you could send this letter on to him? (See letter, enclosed.)

Love, Seamus Todd

They were partly reassured to hear from him, though it was dreadful to think of him imprisoned in the Obelisk of Thunder. The news had affirmed Seamus Todd's story; three of the hostages had been freed.

"We have to do something for him, Mother. He would do the same for us, and he did," said Shannon.

"Honey, there is nothing we can do. This was why I didn't want him to go. Not only is being gay dangerous in that part of the world. What chance has a child like Seamus Todd in the extremely nasty business of Asura politics?"

"But you let him go."

"Yes, I let him go."

"Well, I'm going to the East and help him," said Shannon.

"Dear, there is nothing anyone can do for him. We have to let the government extricate him as best it can."

"I can do something about it. I can rescue him."

"What can you do except be caught yourself?" Asked Caroline.

"I can plead for them to let him go."

"They won't, unless you can offer something in exchange. And I won't hear of you going in his place. That wouldn't give them any advantage except to have two hostages instead of one." Caroline was firm.

"Mom, I can do this."

"Absolutely not. I forbid it."

"When are you going to stop treating me like a child?" Asked Shannon.

"When you stop acting like one."

Naganandini got out of bed and stood on the balcony of her room at Caer Wydr. Since being traded to the Elves, she hadn't been sleeping well. It had nothing to do with the Elves – they had not only been polite, but friendly and hospitable to a fault – it was that she wasn't used to it. Suspicion and paranoia were a way of life in the Obelisk of Thunder, and it was not something easily put aside.

Her body was changing, she could feel it. She could feel the scales spreading across her skin, she was becoming more serpentine each night. For her, it was a sign of power. She would grow stronger, until none could resist her.

There was a knock on the door. "You wanted to see me?"

"Come in, Prince Jason."

"He came halfway into the room and froze before the serpent queen.

"This is what I look like. Every night, I turn into this. Are you afraid?"

"No. I'm not afraid."

"Good, because we have a deal to discuss."

She pulled the belt of her robe more tightly around herself.

"What deal are you willing to make, devil?"

"For the throne. For the throne of the Elves."

"And why do I need your help? I'm next in line for the crown."

"That means nothing. Having the power is the only way. And I can help you become king quickly, in a matter of days or a week instead of months or years. What do you say?" Her tongue flickered.

"How?"

"Marry me."

"And let the old folks step aside? I don't know that my people will accept an Asura as queen."

"They will if they know it means peace between our peoples."

"Is your father likely to do that?"

"We can promise them. Promises are cheap. But when the Regime's forces and the Commonwealth's destroy each other, the two of us will be in position to take over."

Jason rubbed his chin. "Let me think about it. I won't betray my own people."

"You don't need to. All you have to do is trust me."

"They promised to step aside as soon as I married. The king is ill and wants only to retire and rest. I'll let you know."

Shannon took a flight to Beirut, which was the closest her passport could allow. Foreigners were not allowed to fly to Babylon, though they could travel by road. From there, she joined a camel caravan headed to the capital. She was somewhat nervous at first, but the people, the Genies, were kind, and the journey was a pleasant one.

She traded caravans as they came closer to New Babylon. A fat Genie greeted her. "You wish to go to Babylon, my lady?"

"I do."

"We're going that way. You are more than welcome to join us."

She joined the caravan of camels and donkeys, who continued to ply their old trade as they had done for thousands of years.

After a while, she asked the trader, "aren't we going more north than east?"

"Do not worry, my lady. I know what we're doing."

Soon they approached a small town and entered the marketplace.

"Here is where we got off, my lady."

"This doesn't look like Neo-Babylon to me."

"Slaves for sale, slaves!"

She looked back at her guide, who shrugged. "Did you get thirty pieces of silver to betray me?"

He took her by the hand before she could escape. "Don't flatter yourself."

The wedding was as elaborate as Seamus Todd's and Aliyah's. Naganandini looked lovely in a white dress and a train about a block long and carried by sixteen girls. The groom wore his military uniform. They walked to the palace chapel down a street filled with thousands of Elves and representatives from many nations. During the wedding, she refused to look at her new spouse, but no one commented on it.

From the chapel they proceeded to the throne room for the coronation. King Blake and Queen Margaret awaited them, handing over their crowns. Jason was dressed in an ermine robe, a scepter, globe, and anointed with holy oil.

That night, after the feast, they withdrew to the honeymoon suite. A bottle of champagne in ice was waiting for them. She poured them each a glass, and then gave him his. She watched as he drank it slowly.

"Won't you have some, my dear?"

"In a moment."

"Whoa, what a day, I'm feeling a little dizzy."

"Oh? Well, sit down on the bed and rest. Would you like to lay your head in my lap?"

"Thank you, my dear. Mrs. Aldoreth, I should say."

"Queen Aldoreth," she cupped his chin teasingly.

"Will you take a more Elvish name as queen?"

"I think I would prefer to reign under my own name."

"Queen Naganandini? Doesn't quite sound right with "of Tuatha."

"How about Susan?"

"I think that would be fine. Queen Susan."

"They'll learn to love it. Are you all right?"

"Just a – I feel sick."

I'm not surprised. Things are so perfect, I wanted them to end on a high note."

"What have you done?"

"I poisoned your wine."

"You what? Guards!" He tried to call for help but dissolved in a fit of spasms and choking.

"Don't you see this is how it had to be? It's not enough that I be your queen. I must rule the Elves in my own right. It doesn't matter which kingdom I get, as long as I get one. As queen, I will defeat my father's forces and become the most powerful person on earth. And all because of you. I will see that you get a funeral worthy of my first husband. Too bad you won't be here to see it."

"Elves can't. . ." He choked.

"I've taken care of that."

He slumped to the floor, dead.

"Guards, something is wrong with the king. He's having a fit!"

His funeral was as magnificent as the wedding, and much gloomier. It isn't every day the king dies on the same day as his coronation.

"Your majesty, we need to take the body," explained the officer.

"Please, don't. He suffered enough in life. Let me hold onto him in death."

"Your majesty. . ."

"I know an Elf would never request this but I'm not an Elf. He gave his life and his last words were to make sure I inherited the crown in his place. Please stop being mean and trying to take him from me." Naganandini clutched the corpse.

"If you give him to us, we can. . ."

"He doesn't want to. He told me. Please respect my wishes."

"We. . ."

"I insist that his wishes be respected. I am queen now, please do as I ask."

Finally, the officer said, "we'll give you a day to say goodbye. You may remember that your post is not a dictatorship. You can't break the law any more than any of your subjects, and our law says what must be done with a body. It goes to us, no matter what his wishes might have been."

"I have an appointment with my war minister." As soon as the officer was gone, she dropped the corpse.

She met the secretary of war in his office. The Elf first congratulated her on her sudden accession.

"I'll get right to the point. Some of my people are concerned that you will betray us to the Regime, and either try to combine our kingdoms, or subjugate us."

Her smile was meant to be reassuring but was mostly cruel. "Put that thought out of your mind. Nothing would make me happier than to continue the war against my father."

"That is the other concern. The Tuathan army is not your plaything, to be used and thrown away. The monarch has greater power in wartime, but you do not own the kingdom and everything in it like in the Regime. The people here are free citizens, not slaves."

"I have no intention of doing things otherwise. But I will continue to prosecute the war as my predecessors did. We are not going to join the Regime or be crushed by it. We will fight, and I expect you to do your duty, along with all of my soldiers."

"Of course, your Majesty."

That was that. She looked at the mirror with an immense sense of self satisfaction. The world was hers. She had schemed and killed to get it, and now she was about to get revenge on her father and everyone else who had wronged her. Including Seamus Todd, not knowing he had died.

CHAPTER SIX
Glorious Appearing

Aliyah was putting on her makeup when her servant bustled in.

"My lady, the whole castle is talking. Alexis is dead."

"Oh?" She had always hated Alexis. Still, she was not inclined to gloat, and held her reaction in case he wasn't really dead.

"Seamus Todd. . ."

"What? Where is he now?"

"Probably in the morgue, mistress. But you mustn't go in there after him. My lady, what are you doing?"

"I have to see him. I have to find out."

He was indeed in the mortuary. So was Alexis. And two dead guards. She glanced at the Duke to make sure he was dead and nodded in satisfaction to see his mangled body. Then she slapped him just to make sure he was dead. He was. She rushed to Seamus Todd's side.

"You were my only friend here," she said softly. "We talked about escape, but I knew they were just dreams. There's no way out of here for you and me. Except one, and you've already taken it."

Her eyes brimmed with tears as she touched his pale skin. She saw his scars, the Celtic cross on his left cheek. He was even more beautiful in death than in life, she thought. She took his hand.

She washed the body and arrayed it in a wrap. As she turned him on his back, she saw what he had kept hidden from the world. "So, Elves do have wings." They were like a butterfly's, white and green, and she didn't see how he kept them tucked away like he did.

She didn't know how long she sat there in silent communion with the corpse. It was at least twenty minutes. Then she pulled her hand away. How strange, she thought, my hands must have warmed his, because it returned the warmth. She took his other hand from where it lay across his chest.

It was warm, too.

"Seamus Todd, Seamus Todd, wake up, if you can hear me!"

He gasped for breath. His eyes fluttered open, then squeezed shut against the light.

"Hold on, I'll get a doctor."

Cold.

So very cold.

And deep and dark. He wasn't sure where he was, maybe in an elevator, because he felt himself going up. Out of the cold and dark, back to the light.

The room swam into view. He looked at the overhead light and turned away. I'm alive, he thought. And I'm going to kill Alexis.

He rested, conserving his strength. He was enervated, weak, but his strength was slowly increasing. His wings beat. He felt the outline of one, delicately. The transparent wings he'd had all his life had been replaced by larger and more colorful ones, proof that he had indeed died and returned to life.

He looked around and saw Alexis' body. At least he was dead, too. But being a demon, he wasn't coming back. And he was robbed of his revenge.

He half climbed, half fell off the autopsy table, and staggered into the bathroom.

Seamus Todd looked at himself in the mirror. His face was marred by scars.

In his frustration he slammed the mirror. It cracked. He hit it again, and it shattered into a thousand pieces all over the floor. Looking down on them, he could see his shattered visage in its fragments.

The boy opened the medicine cabinet and brought out a roll of gauze. He wrapped his face in it, making a mask for himself. Then there was a knock on the door.

"Seamus Todd?"

"Yes?"

"You're alive."

"Thanks to you. No thanks to Alexis."

"I brought a doctor. Come sit down and let him examine you."

He followed them into the autopsy room.

"Actually, it was Pryadar that saved you," Aliyah said.

"He did? I think I remember seeing something – something horrible."

"You saw Pryadar's night form? What does he look like?"

"Like a giant spider."

"Really?"

"I don't kid about food or giant spiders."

"Well, don't ever let him know you know what he looks like. I can't imagine dying is much fun, even if you got better."

"It's not. I don't intend on dying, ever again."

"What about the wings?"

"We're all born with transparent wings. When we return, we get our second pair. And if we die again, we have eagle's wings."

They're lovely. How does it work?"

"You see, some of the DNA that went into Elves includes butterflies, eagles, and a kind of jellyfish."

"The immortal ones?"

It took a lot of research, but scientists had figured out how to duplicate it. An Elf could live forever, for in dying, their stem cells reactivate. But most die after fifteen hundred years. Then cell death catches up and begins to age them. And each time they return, they grow stronger.

"I see. How do they die?"

"I'm not sure. I think we choose to. To keep us dead, though, there are ways. One way I know of is to dump us off into space. If we don't have a world to settle on, we don't recover. Another way is to be instantly disintegrated by a laser."

"How come other people haven't been able to duplicate it, then?"

"I don't know. All of the seven Peoples have had their DNA tampered with. They may simply be other combinations."

"But to raise from the dead. No other people can do that."

"Maybe the Elves destroyed the formula so it couldn't be replicated."

Aliyah said, "you would think they would try."

"That's probably where the ghouls came from."

That was right. An attempt to restore life, using the space virus, led to the creation of the zombies. They couldn't quite get it right, but they came close.

"And once they got a result, they had to live with it. It was too late when their experiment didn't work. You can't kill someone to see if they'll recover," Seamus Todd said.

"Sure we can, but I understand what you mean."

"We have immortality, but not freedom from pain. Without that, it can easily become a curse."

"Asuras and Elves live a long time anyway, much longer than us Genies."

"How long?" Seamus Todd asked.

"An Asura can live eight hundred years. Demons live for less than a hundred years."

"And Genies?" Asked Seamus Todd.

"About two hundred years."

"Well, that's pretty good. I mean, we just have to settle for the lives we have."

"So says the virtually immortal."

"If you do it right, once should be enough."

"You don't have to worry about dying."

"But I do. I have no idea how many times I can live again. An Elf in the last century died seven times for his country. He wasted his lives."

"I wouldn't say that was a waste."

"Maybe not."

"That's why the Asuras have never been able to defeat you. Your numbers are much fewer than ours, but endlessly replaceable. Then we should stop attacking you."

"Yes. The only way to defeat us is to do it all at once. Elves have to be around to bring the others back."

"And the reason is – dare I say it – love."

"Yes," said Seamus Todd.

"It must be nice."

"Look, don't blame me for who I am. If it was up to me, we would all live together happily, forever."

"I'm not blaming you," said Aliyah. "I'm just wondering."

They helped him back to his room. Two servants had just started cleaning in preparation for redecorating, but

Seamus Todd explained, "the rumors of my demise are greatly exaggerated."

They fled in terror, and Seamus Todd collapsed into his bed. He would need a lot of rest over the next couple of days.

Immortality

Elvish cells have an incredible ability to regenerate. When an Elf dies, their stem cells work quickly to repair the damage and then revive the Elf. The scientific research took away the permanence of death, but could not remove pain, and as can be seen in Seamus Todd's case, the repairs are sometimes imperfect. In his example, he developed epileptic symptoms, and the damage to his face, though partially repaired, was not complete. Advances in medical research, however, have assured a complete recovery. It helps if people gather to love the decedent to recover more quickly. They also have incredible stamina, and though they enjoy food and drink, can go for long periods on just water. Faced with overwhelming odds, they can go into a vegetative state until things are more congenial.

When an Elf decides it is time to die, which is usually when they have lived about fifteen hundred years, they may choose death in space, since they cannot revive beyond Earth's atmosphere; death by laser, which disrupts the cells beyond repair, or least frequently, radiation. Because of their devotion to strict population control, the number of Elves has remained at about three million for millennia. An Elf has to die before a new one can be born.

News of Seamus Todd's death had been sent swiftly to Caer Wydr, the Elvish capital. King Blake was somber as he read the news to his people.

"It is with a heavy heart that I announce my grandson, Seamus Todd McKenzie, died. One of the Emperor's retainers put him to death while in Asura custody. The functionary who killed him has also been killed, but that will not bring him back to life.

"What will bring him back is thinking about and loving him. Picture him and think good thoughts, and he will recover faster. It is sad enough he must remain a hostage to the Asuras.

"Queen Margaret and I have agreed to the accession of Jason the First and Susan the Second as reigning queen of Tuatha. Everyone please do your best to follow her and keep Tuatha united and strong.

"We have asked to step in and take the royal throne back but are disinclined to turn back the clock. Instead, let us go forward, at least until the supreme court decides whether her accession is legal. We will not oppose it and we ask that all our people support her as they have supported us for the last thousand years. This is my final public broadcast as king emeritus. My queen and I will be retiring to Iberia to spend the rest of our days in peace and quiet. To younger and stronger shoulders, we commend the future."

When he first saw Pryadar again, he wondered if he was joking around. His eyes grew wide, his jaw dropped, and he backed away. His terror seemed genuine. Unlike Aliyah, though, he already knew very well that Elves don't stay dead.

"I'm sorry I scared you, your Majesty."

"I'm sorry I worried you. It's just – could you stand a little further away? I am nervous when I'm around dead things."

"But I'm not dead."

"You were."

"I'm still the same person. Only. . ."

He blinked. "What happened," asked Pryadar.

"I seem to have developed epilepsy from my experience. I don't know if it's seizures or something else, but it came back from the dead with me."

"There, there, lad." He embraced him in his six fold grip. "It'll be all right. There are treatments for it, you know. We'll take you to the best doctors in the realm. And maybe plastic surgeons as well." He touched his chin. "Oh, look at you."

"I'm all right, your majesty." He rubbed his face across the bandage.

"I feel horrible about what happened. Is there any way I can make it up to you? Is there anything in all my wide realm you might like to have as your own?"

"Well, I've always been interested in seeing the seven wonders. The oldest ones are the pyramids."

"Well, let's go see them then."

There had been many lists for the seven wonders in the last five millennia. Besides the pyramids, the latest list included;

- the statue of Eon at Helsinki,
- the Taj Mahal,
- the great Buddha in Shang province in China,
- the Sculpture of Crazy Horse, which should be almost finished,
- the great zoo in Cologne, where extinct creatures had been reproduced through DNA,
- the castle at Caer Wydr,
- and the Obelisk of Thunder in Babylon.

They arrived at Gaza in less than an hour. People looked amazed to see Pryadar, an Elf at his side, touring the pyramids.

"Wow, they're beautiful," said Seamus Todd.

"My father had them restored before you were born. Before that, they were looking pretty ragged."

The granite pyramids had been covered in shining white limestone, as they had originally been built. Then the largest, Menes' tomb, had been rebuilt as a step pyramid, with greenery on three levels, eternally watered by an irrigation system. A golden cap crowned the pyramid, which again reached its original height. They started walking up the steps, conversing in low tones.

Without a word, the crowd passed to let them through. Their three headed king, accompanied by a horribly scarred Elf wrapped up like a mummy, was more than they had hoped to see in coming to Gaza.

They admire you, lord."

"And next week they'll be revolting. I don't trust them. I never can."

"Well, you can trust me."

"I'd like to think so."

"Your majesty, I am yours. And when an Elf is loyal, they are loyal all the way to death."

"I know. I wish my people were so loyal. All they do is rebel against me."

"Well, if you do your best, there's nothing to complain about."

"Demons and Genie know only the whip. If you are not firm with them, they break out in riots and revolt."

They didn't in Tuatha, he thought, but said nothing. "Look, there's the Sphinx."

"It's been refurbished, too. I wanted to ask you, how does your king keep the people's loyalty?"

"Our people obey out of love."

"I have tried to show them love, tried to earn their loyalty. All they ever do is rebel, forcing me to exert control, which makes them rebel still more."

"Your majesty, I don't have any answers. I'm only a boy. The kinds of problems you face are beyond my meager comprehension."

Pryadar nodded but said nothing.

"Elves don't act like this. Elves are peace-loving, hard-working, responsible citizens and artists. We don't have as many ups and downs as other people."

"Maybe it's because of your long lives. You have less to lose. Or more to lose, so you guard it more preciously. If only I'd been born king of the Elves instead of the Asuras."

"We're more intense, I guess. But fate made you a king. You must try to do the best you can do. That's all anybody can do."

"Thank you, lad."

"Besides, you've got one Elf follower who is grateful to you. You saved my life."

"Oh. Do you remember seeing me when I came in?"

"No," he lied.

"Good. I'm glad to hear that."

"Thank you, your majesty." Seamus Todd looked away.

"What is wrong."

"Well, you killed Alexis. I know you did it for me. . ."

"That's right."

"But it was still murder. And if I replace him in your affections, how do I know you won't get rid of me when the time is right?"

"Am I likely to catch you torturing someone?"

"No."

"Well, there you are then. I did the greatest thing I could do in this life. I killed for you."

The greatest thing anyone can do is die for you, not kill for you, Seamus Todd was thoughtful. Yes, he had killed his torturer, but murder was still murder. And murderers can't be trusted. "Let me think about this awhile, my lord, if I may."

"Of course, lad. It is likely, if you give your loyalty to me, that you will be next in line for the throne."

They came to the top of the pyramid and rested in the shade of the golden peak. A cart came past, offering ice cream, sodas and drinks. Pryadar bought some for both of them, and leaned back, looking north over his kingdom.

"Have you ever come here with your own kids?"

"No."

"They would have had fun."

"Naganandini wouldn't have fun, and she would ruin it for everybody," Pryadar said.

"But she's your daughter."

"I don't need a daughter. I need an heir."

"But me, lord. I'm just an Elf, and I've been – damaged."

"You need not be physically perfect to assume the throne, but we will see what our plastic surgeons can do. You have to think bigger than that. My boy, you have great potential. Let me teach you everything I know. My people would accept an Elf as king, they're partial to long reigns. Yours would be the longest in history."

"I admit the offer is tempting. Who wouldn't want to rule the most powerful kingdom on earth? I could make peace with the Elves, change the laws, make. . ."

"What, lad?"

"Nothing, I was just daydreaming. It's just that. . ."

"What?" Asked Pryadar.

"I'm not sure."

"Well, when you are sure, come to me."

Seamus Todd found himself drawing closer and closer to Pryadar the Spider. His admiration for the man persisted, in spite of his obvious flaws. He had charisma, and Seamus Todd thought he could see the sensitive person hidden under the public persona of ruthless efficiency. As they headed down the steps, Pryadar explained, "we'd like you to do some work for us."

"Certainly, your majesty."

"What do you know about the law?"

Asura Society

Compare the egalitarian Elves with the strict castes of Asura society, similar to the system of India. Asuras occupy the top caste and are almost worshiped as gods. Asuras might have different numbers of eyes, heads, arms, legs or other bodily differences. Less than one percent of the population controls ninety percent of the power and wealth.

Demons or Rakshasas occupy the next highest caste. They far outnumber the Asuras but have been programmed to look upon the Asuras as gods and masters. They cannot tolerate sunlight and if exposed, turn hard like stone.

The Genies occupy the lowest caste. Though it is technically their land, they have been oppressed by the Asuras and Demons for over a century. Their lives are shorter than Asuras, but longer than demons. Several generations might pass under the same Asura ruler, leading to their godly image. Genies turn visibly different colors according to their emotions, such as red for rage and golden for joy. They have more color cells in their skin than most people.

"Virtually nothing, my lord." Elf laws tended to be simple and direct, since nobody ever broke the law there anyway. In Asura law, by contrast, there was a huge body of work, more than one person could read in a lifetime. All boiling down to one simple principle; thou shalt not defy those who have more power than you.

"We'd like you to work on some cases for us."

"As a clerk?"

"As a judge."

"A judge? Your majesty, I don't know anything about being a judge." Sure, it was something he'd often wondered about, but knew the reality was nothing like a fantasy. Real people's lives depended on judicial decisions.

"Maybe someday, after I've finished law school or. . ."

"Monday," he said firmly. "You start being a judge on Monday."

"Very well, my lord."

His first case was a boy even younger than Seamus Todd. He wondered how a child this age could have done anything. On the other hand, Asura law was often designed to free those guilty of enormities and crush minor offenders. He looked like a typical Genie, with light brown skin and dark hair. And a thousand years of pain in his eyes. Head downcast, he stood before the Elf.

"Your honor, this boy killed his father with malice aforethought, because he wouldn't buy him an expensive toy."

"That's not what happened, your honor," said the boy's lawyer. "What happened is a child got hold of a dangerous toy and killed the one he loved most."

"I didn't mean to kill him. It was an accident. Please, I feel bad enough I killed my dad."

"Tell me what happened," Seamus Todd said.

They had gone shopping that morning, and the boy had seen an Elven game technology device called a Mongoose, the latest in simulated electronic games. Seamus Todd sympathized. He wanted one, too.

"My father said I'd have to save my money and we'd see about getting it later."

"When they got home, his dad took out his gun and started cleaning it. He left it out, and the boy picked it up and looked at it. Then his dad came in, saw him with the gun, charged in, shouting "no," and he pulled the trigger. Dad fell to the floor."

"I find the defendant not guilty. This was a horrible tragic accident."

"Well done, lad," Emperor Harsha appeared at his elbow.

"You were watching?"

"On the closed circuit the whole time. I thought you handled it very well. And you followed the law."

Seamus Todd would have been prouder if it hadn't felt like something Kefka had written,

Excitedly, he told Aliyah about his tenure as a judge.

"Harsha said he was proud of me. I hope Pryadar is proud of me, too."

"So, you're getting on well with him."

"I sure am."

"I wouldn't be handling it so well if I were you," said Aliyah.

"Handling what?"

"Your deformity."

"The fact that I got mangled? Alexis did it because he thought he could get away with it."

"Pryadar was behind it."

"What?"

"Pryadar ordered the attack," Aliyah said.

"I don't believe it."

"Ask him."

Seamus Todd said, "he saved me. He came bursting through the door and rescued me."

"How did he know where you were?"

"I guess he sent me down there, but. . ."

"Yes. I suppose he had people meet you in the casbah, too, who were in desperate need of his mercy?"

"He set me up, didn't he," he realized.

"I'm afraid he did."

Seamus Todd asked, "what am I going to do?"

"I don't know."

"I mean, I'm going to get even."

"How?"

"I don't know yet."

"I have an idea," said Aliyah.

"About revenge?"

"I'll lure him to my room in the middle of the night. He'll take it as an invitation. You'll be waiting to trap him."

"All right."

He went to the armory.

"Welcome, my lord," the bored looking man got off his stool at the sight of him and hurried over.

"What have you got?"

"Well, there's this modification on your brace. It has a laser pointer, and then fires a bolt of energy."

He didn't say anything.

After a moment, the clerk came around the desk for the first time.

"My lord?"

"What happened?"

"You seem to have wandered off for a moment."

He shook his head. "I'm fine. I'll take this."

He ran to the harem, where he heard voices. He was just in time.

"I don't mean to hurt you, my dear." Pryadar.

"Please just leave me alone."

He burst in through the curtain. Pryadar was there in his monster spider form, towering over Aliyah. She wasn't a completely helpless female; she had drawn a dagger. The great dome of Pryadar's many eyed head turned toward the door which was partly lost in shadow.

"Who's there?"

"Seamus Todd." He raised his gauntlet and aimed a targeting laser right at one of the enemy's eyes.

"What are you doing?"

"Do what you have to do," said Aliyah.

And reality blinked again. He woke from the seizure to the monster bearing down on him. He managed to squeeze off one shot.

It went wide, but it brought half the roof crashing down. Through a thick pall of white dust, he saw Pryadar was pinned by debris.

"Help me!"

"I'm going to stun you. You'll still be able to talk."

"Get me out of here."

"Do you understand?"

"Yes."

He reached down and stunned him. "Now, did you give Alexis permission to torture me."

"He was only supposed to question you and threaten you with torture. Then I would rush in and save you from him."

"Oh?"

"But my plan didn't work. I was delayed, and then I transmogrified as you see me now."

"Why?"

"Because I was tired of Alexis and his scheming and backbiting. I wanted a servant I could trust, one who was capable of supreme loyalty, like an Elf. I thought if I charged in at the last second and saved you, your loyalty would be assured."

"Why didn't you just ask me?"

"If I had to ask, I could never be sure of your devotion. Actions speak louder than words."

"They sure do. Did you see what he did to me?"

"I know it was horrible. I don't want to see it."

Seamus Todd peeled away the bandages to reveal his face.

"I said I didn't want to see." His many unblinking eyes were fixed on him.

"Why not? It's your handiwork, you created it."

"You think you're damaged." He rolled over and revealed his back.

"Oh, my. Yuck." Seamus Todd's lip curled in disgust. His back was infested. There were large white grubs, scuttling beetles, and worst of all, pale worms that seemed to write in syncopation. "How can you allow yourself to suffer so horribly for no reason."

"There is no undeserved suffering. Every life form is sacred."

"Except human life. What about your life?"

"It is the mark of suffering that must be borne. Alexis went too far. I never meant for you to get hurt, I promise you."

"To promise is to lie. But you meant to kill Alexis."

"Yes, I had thought about it for months. He was plotting against me."

"Good for him. That's what you deserve. To spend every day looking over your shoulder, wondering who will betray you next. Well, I can tell you who is plotting against you now."

"No, please. I will release the hostages."

"Really?"

"I will stop the war. Only let me live."

"Command it, then. We will go to your screen and do it now."

"As you say."

A great claw raised its way out of the wreck. Aliyah slashed at it with her dagger. It went flying, and Pryadar screamed. It was the worst sound he'd ever heard. The stench of blood filled the air, as his black blood went gushing down into pools on the dusty floor.

"Please, mercy, lord," he raised a bloody stump.

"Kill him, said Aliyah. "It's nothing he didn't do to you."

"No. I can't kill him like this, even if he is the monster on the outside he is on the inside."

"He'll kill you if you don't."

"Are the hostages freed?"

"Yes."

"Will you end the war?"

"Yes, I agree, anything," he shuddered.

"Aliyah, go get him help."

"You're crazy."

"Having experienced death myself, I have a little more perspective on it than I did before. I'm not going to kill him."

She left.

Seamus Todd lowered his weapon.

"You're weak," said Pryadar. He started to crawl forward.

The weapon came up again, and he grew still. "Don't move. I'll wrap your hand. Just remember, I could have killed you any time."

"But you didn't."

"Be quiet. I know how to use this." He took a part of the silk curtain and bound his arm.

"You will live to regret this, boy. I should kill you over and over again, until you beg for death. I should tear you to pieces."

"Yeah, well. That's the difference between humans and brutes," said Seamus Todd. "Animals are grateful."

"Grateful! You should be grateful to me. I saved your life."

"You ruined my life."

"That was not part of my plan."

"What was your plan?"

"To burst in and save you and end up killing Alexis."

"Why?"

"Because I knew I couldn't rely on him anymore. He has always been treacherous, dangerous, and cruel. I needed a servant I could rely on, someone who was not always seeking to supplant me. You. . ."

"Well, it turned out you can't trust anyone. Because you're the one who can't be trusted."

"Do you think I don't know that?"

They went to Pryadar's office and he dialed up his army commander.

"End the attack. No more war. We're rolling it up."

"My lord, are you sure? We're only ten miles from the border."

"Yes, I am sure. Stop the war. That is an order from the commander in chief."

"As you command, my lord."

The guards came into the room just then, gathered them both up, and escorted them to the Emperor's court room.

"What has been going on?" asked Harsha.

"He attacked me," explained Seamus Todd.

"He dared lift his hand against my royal personage."

"That was because you attacked me first."

"I said the Elf was not to be harmed. Under whose authority was he mistreated?"

137

"Mine, Father," said Pryadar sulkily.

"I told you not to."

"I didn't intend things to go so far. Alexis exceeded his orders. I was going to burst in at the opportune moment and save the boy."

"Why didn't you?"

"I was delayed."

"Pryadar, playing with people's lives is wrong, whether you arrive in time or not," said the old Emperor. "We have discussed this with you before."

"He promised to end the war," added Seamus Todd.

"Under duress."

"Then it will be done. Call back our troops."

"It is already done, sire."

"Very well."

"I lied to get away from him. He was frightening me."

"Oh, grow up. Stop whining."

"I was scared. Dead people scare me. . ."

"Enough."

"This isn't over," said Pryadar.

Glaring daggers at each other, they each retired to their rooms.

Perhaps he had gone too far, but he was just so angry. Perhaps he had even blown the chance to become heir, but it had been a narrow chance, anyway. Elves are brave loyal friends or fierce enemies. Elves will go to great lengths for revenge, though they have to be really provoked.

CHAPTER SEVEN

Exile

For a while, everything returned to its normal routine. He continued to go to assassin school. He and Aliyah continued to discuss plans for an escape. Pryadar seemed to be avoiding him. Seamus Todd began to make plans to return to Tuatha and a normal life. He was always prepared for battle, though, and kept his gauntlet. He slept with his arm around it.

Things changed in one night in winter. Seamus Todd was awakened by guards in the night and hurried to the throne room at about two in the morning. They hadn't attacked him, so he didn't use his gauntlet, but held onto it closely.

"What's going on?" He asked.

Nobody answered.

The Emperor was escorted in by a retinue of soldiers. Then Pryadar came in and sat on the throne of state.

"My son, what is going on?" Asked the Emperor. Other people began to assemble, wondering about this odd turn of events.

"Well, you see, dad, what's going on is called a coup de 'tat. It means you are no longer Emperor. And I am. My generals support me in this." He waved a hand at the men assembled before him. "And I have you to thank," he turned to Seamus Todd.

"Me?"

"Yes, you. It was you who inspired me to do this. Why should I be sitting in a corner waiting for him to die, when I should be Emperor?"

"My son, please do not do this. Terrible things happen when the law of succession is broken. And that is what you are doing."

"What I'm doing is taking my rightful place. Your reign is over, old man. No one's taking notice of you anymore."

"Pryadar, please. You're not ready."

"And when will I be ready, do you think?"

"At the rate you are going, never."

"Exactly. You want to keep me from the throne, so I stole it."

"No, I wanted you to be ready. All your life, I have tried to teach you the king's first duty is to his people. You have never listened. You think as Emperor you will do whatever you want to do. You don't understand that the least peasant has more freedom than you."

"So, you've told me. So you've told me over and over and over again."

"Because you haven't been listening. A king must do what the law says, whether he agrees with it or not."

"And if I don't like the law, I'll change it."

"You can't do that."

"I can do anything I wish. I am supreme. Do you see this crown? My crown. That gives me power to do whatever I want."

"That crown is nothing but an illusion. It is the welfare of the people that must come first."

"If they don't do what I want, I'll crush them under my boot. I've seen your style and I despise it. You are too soft on them, too tenderhearted. You funnel money that could be spent on the military or for better uses and squander it on the idle poor. Well, no more. If I have to, I will turn this country into a giant barracks, where every man, woman, and child is enlisted in the army. There will be no stepping out of line. They will do what they're told, when they're told. Just see if they get away with being insolent to me, then. I'll crush them like the insects they are.

"No more of your generosity, no more mercy. I have seen these things to their rotten core, and I hate them. Anyone who defies me finds their way to the chopping block in an hour. I intend to streamline the entire system until it works like a gun in my hand. And when I get done bringing this nation to heel, I'll finish the war with the Elves. There will not be one left alive on Earth before my rule is over. If they return a million times, I will destroy them a million and one."

"You will only increase the rebellions against yourself."

"Then I will crush them and turn their lands over to those who are loyal."

"That will be a small number indeed."

"So be it. If I have to have only a handful of men I can trust, so much the better. They either obey or die, those are their choices. I have no problem sentencing rebellious subjects to death. In fact, I prefer it. Fewer mouths to feed, and more for the army and the police force. "My father whipped you with whips, but I will whip you with scorpions."

Aliyah came in just then.

"You. I haven't forgotten who severed my hand. I'll deal with you soon enough. As for you, father, I sentence you to exile. You have ten days to be out of the Regime, or I'll have you put to death."

"Where will I go, my son?"

"I don't care! Go anywhere, you have the freedom you so longed for. You're the freest man in the realm, because you are the one person who can survive as a beggar. Everybody else will fall into step, but I will let you go. For ten days, anyway. Go to the Elves, go to the East. I don't care. But if I find you in my kingdom in ten days, your head will be displayed on a post like a common criminal."

"Alas. I am nothing but a poor old man. If you do this to your own father, what will you do to your subjects?"

"Is there anyone here who wants to go with this pathetic old man? Go ahead, I won't stop you. Anyone?"

"I will."

"Who said that?" He looked around, almost unable to believe what he heard.

"I will," said Seamus Todd again.

"Seamus Todd, no!" Said Aliyah. "No one can take the part of someone out of favor. It's bad luck even to look on someone cursed by a king."

"I don't care. Look at him, a poor old man. He's already broken, what more do you want? I'm not going to just stand by and do nothing."

"You can't. You are pledged to remain here."

"You said I could go."

"I didn't expect you to volunteer. You're a hostage. And I certainly wasn't expecting anybody to join him."

"Well, they're not Elves, are they?"

"If you do this, you can only stay with him until the old man dies. Then you must return to the obelisk."

"Yes."

"Promise me then."

"To promise is to lie. I said I would do it. "That which I will perform, I will do it, ere I speak." He's quoting Cordelia, King Lear, Act I, scene 1.

"Take him and go. Get out of my sight, traitor. This is goodbye. I will never look on your misshapen face again."

Harsha spoke up. "He should have been my son instead of you. The Elf was more my grandson than any of you." He turned to Seamus Todd. "I can't let you do it, Ravana."

"Well, I'm going to. Your step will falter less if there is someone to guide you."

"My son." Harsha embraced him.

Pryadar said, "you both make me sick. Get out of here now. Tonight."

A courtier spoke up for them. "My lord, you mustn't do this."

"Then you are banished, too. As is anyone else who takes the side of that cursed man."

Harsha started to say, "your majesty. . ."

"I have already spoken. I have had enough from you. I may have let you get away with so much because you were my father, but no more. Enough. You don't seem to understand the situation. I am in charge here. This kingdom does not belong to you anymore."

"It belongs to neither of us, it belongs to the people."

"I am the people. Me! I am! There will be only one vote and one voter. No meaningful difference exists between me and the state. I am the state, the law, and the public. I will restore the Regime to greatness once more."

"You're out of your mind."

"Your majesty, it doesn't matter. Let him have his moment," Seamus Todd said. "It won't be a long reign, thanks to nobody but himself. Let's walk out of here with your dignity intact."

"You're right, of course, my boy. Come, let's be gone."

"Just a moment. We don't want you two getting separated. Chain them together."

A guard came forward and handcuffed them together on a long chain.

"Now drop them off in the desert to die."

The guards bundled them into the elevator, down to the garage, and into a waiting car.

Exile

Seamus Todd's offer to go along with Harsha into exile was completely unexpected, because by Asura standards it was completely dishonorable. No person of the Regime, whether Demon, Asura, or Genie, would have done such a thing. Seamus Todd was unaware of what was at stake. He simply saw a chance to help someone he saw as pitiful, and at the same time escape a perilous situation. In allowing Seamus Todd to go, Pryadar might have been treating him with the contempt he felt was deserved.

"We must be careful, my prince," said the Emperor. "Babylon is more dangerous by night than by day."

He nodded but couldn't see anything dangerous as they passed through the dark streets. Nobody was about. He wondered where the people all went. Hopefully they went to their nice cozy homes like people in Europe, and did whatever made them happy.

Drowsy, he started to doze.

A noise woke him up. He thought at first it was thunder, but as he woke up more, he realized it might have been a laser blast. He started, as something hit the car, or they ran over something.

"Keep going, please," said the Emperor. He sounded a little afraid, making Seamus Todd wonder what was happening.

The driver ignored him and got out. The street was silent. In the distance, a garbage can burned.

"We really shouldn't be stopping," the old man shook his head.

The guard seemed to be listening for sounds of pursuit. He must have heard what he was searching for or something, because he turned white and fled back the way they came.

"We've got to find a place to hide," the Emperor said.

Suddenly, a sound. It was somewhere between a howl of pain and a scream of rage.

"It's a wilding."

"What should we do?"

"Hide."

They hid. Behind some garbage cans. Soon the Demons came into sight. There were Demons of every size, shape and description. They seemed to run in eerie slow motion, as they turned the corner, rolled onward and disappeared into the darkness. The dim light was illuminated by the red glow of their eyes.

"What are they looking for?"

"Us."

"Specifically?"

"Anyone they can find."

"What should we do?"

"We can either try to walk and hope they don't find us, or we can stay here and wait until dawn."

"It can't be much longer." They remained in hiding. More than once, they heard screams, and worse than screams.

"I'm going to see if the car will start."

"I don't think that's a good idea."

"It's just a matter of time until they find us. I think we have to try to outrun them."

He tinkered with the car for a minute, and got it running again. He and the Emperor climbed in as fast as they could, and they took off.

"They're coming."

They were. A mob of howling demons were coming down the street after them. They got closer than he would have liked before he managed to pull ahead.

Seamus Todd drove through the night. By noon the next day, they reached the great black wall of the city. Its gate faced north. They joined the traffic queue of people flowing in and out. Camels, mules and cattle mixed with wheeled vehicles and flying vehicles, because the city was a no-fly zone. They passed through the portal and into the suburbs in the surrounding area.

It was a relief to get through the gate and away from the madding crowd, but the suburbs around the walled city were nearly as creepy. They were empty.

"What happened here?"

"My son's reavers came here, collecting for the army."

"What about the women and children?"

"They were taken, too. The children to carry supplies, the women, to serve the men."

"Oh, no."

"I'm sorry, son, it happens."

"Maybe we should find a place to sleep and start fresh tomorrow."

"First, can we take this thing off?" He indicated the manacle. "It's starting to chafe."

Seamus Todd searched for a tool shed that was open. He finally found one with a laser saw. A quick snap and they were free of each other. Then he used it to cut the cuffs away.

"You've done enough for me, my boy. You may go now, if you wish."

"You're letting me go?"

"I won't need any more help where I'm going."

"And where are you going?" Asked Seamus Todd.

The Emperor was silent.

"Are you thinking about killing yourself, sir? I better stay with you awhile. I'm going home to Tuatha, and you're welcome to come home with me."

"Are you kidding?"

"I don't kid about food or sticking together."

"I don't think I'd be welcome there."

"Nonsense. We accept refugees from the Regime all the time."

"I'm an old deposed monarch," said Harsha

"You'll be all right."

"Nothing but an old despot."

"No, your majesty. You were a good king and a good father. You can't help the way things turned out," explained the Elf.

"Thank you, my boy. We'll go to Tuatha. I'll give it a try."

They went into the nearest house and found some bedrooms. They slept the rest of the day and the next night. Amazingly, for the first time since the home invasion, he slept soundly. In the morning, they went through the food storage units and found enough food for two or three days. They then headed out, northwest in the primitive car.

They passed through the suburbs. It seemed something survived in the abandoned village after all. An old man, possibly as old as the Emperor, came out of hiding.

"Here, take this," said Harsha.

"Why did you give him money? We might need that before we get home."

"Don't you know what charity is, my boy?"

"Yes, it's helping people in trouble. But the ones in the most trouble is us."

"It's a duty to look out for the less fortunate."

"We have to save our money." It was simply a situation with which he was not familiar. There were no poor or outcast Elves, so he had never learned about almsgiving.

The next day, they were approaching what he thought was an ancient tel, when the car began to sputter. He quickly pulled over and looked under the hood.

"The exofibulator's belt is broken. If we had another belt, we could probably repair it," explained Seamus Todd. Though not in his brother Christian's league, he was a fair mechanic, and could handle most things.

"This isn't the best place to break down."

"Where are we?"

"This is the junk yard for old spaceships."

"Really? You guys have a junk yard of space ships?"

"Yes. I'm sorry. I know this is no place to break down."

"Are you kidding? For me, this is paradise."

He went scrambling through the ruins. The wreck of a Scorpion X-1S towered ominously over everything. There was a Dragonfly to the left, a Hellstorm to the right. It was fun, climbing in and out of the wrecks, imagining the stories that went with each vessel. There must have been over a hundred, most of which were Elven ships captured.

He realized they were kept instead of being recycled because they were reverse engineered. The Asuras copied the designs of Elven ships into their own machines in the ever-escalating arms race. The Elves probably had to do the same.

He looked up, startled. There was a noise.

"Who's there?"

Someone or something moved in the junk, and he was sure it wasn't the Emperor.

"Hyah!"

It was a young Genie with jet black hair, with a scarf up to his freckled nose. He wielded a long piece of metal as if it were a club.

"What are you doing here?"

"I live here. What are you doing here?"

"Looking around."

"I'm a robber."

"Are you supposed to just announce it like that?"

"I guess not. Hand over your money."

"I don't have any," explained Seamus Todd. Which was true. The Emperor carried their small amount of money.

"That's all right. We'll have to fight."

"Is everybody down here crazy? I just came to get a belt."

"That's the idea."

"All right." He held up his gauntlet.

What are you going to do with that?"

Seamus Todd pointed and let off a laser blast into the nearest pile of tires. They exploded in a burst of dust and debris.

"Wow. That's pretty impressive. I'm afraid I'm no match for you."

"Won't you join us for lunch?"

"I can't eat with my enemies."

"Just for the moment, we don't have to be enemies. I'm Seamus Todd."

"I'm Rory."

He did look hungry. In fact, he might have been starving.

They went back to the car and spread out a picnic lunch. Afterwards, they looked until they found a belt that at least might get them to the next town. Seamus Todd installed it with some help from Rory.

"Come with us." It would be nice to have someone his own age along, besides the old Emperor.

"I don't know."

"It's better than living all alone in the junk. What happened to your parents? Don't you have any family?"

The reavers came and took them three days ago. They told me to hide."

"So, you came here?"

"There was nowhere else to go."

"We're on the trail of the reavers. Perhaps we can find your family."

"That would be nice."

"We're heading to Tuatha. There's room for one more," said the Emperor. "If you like, I will make you one of my retainers."

The three of them climbed in and headed off.

Finally, they came to a village and took the car to a mechanic for a serious look over. The belt was replaced, and the engine checked out. Though old, it was in good working order.

They were interrupted when a great brute holding a heavy sword stepped forward. "All right, all you peasants, line up. In the Emperor's name, you will join his army and fight for your country."

The Emperor stepped forward. "Isn't it interesting, then, that I don't remember any such order?"

"Your majesty," quavered the officer. "On your knees, all of you. The Emperor is here."

Everyone fell prostrate, leaving only the Emperor and Seamus Todd standing.

"Your grace, forgive me, I only followed orders."

"Then follow this one. I think we've had enough of the recruiters. Go on back to the army and serve your country well."

"Yes, your majesty, thank you." He hurried away.

"It seems I have missed much in being Emperor. Beggars and people being shanghaied into the army."

"And now, slavery."

"Pryadar wouldn't bring that back, would he?"

"He already did."

"Well, if you think slavery is wrong. . ."

"Of course, slavery is wrong. If you think begging is bad, I wish you could see what it's like to be a slave."

"As for the slaves, we will see about that."

"Where are we going?"

"To the slave market."

As soon as they saw the old king, people started bowing.

"Slavery has been outlawed in this district."

The slaves and many of the people cheered. The slavers looked wrathful but resigned. As the prisoners were freed, one of them ran up to Seamus Todd.

"Elf, are you Seamus Todd McKenzie?"

"Yes, yes, I am."

"Your sister was here."

"Which one? Siobhan or Shannon?"

"Shannon."

"What on earth was she doing here?"

"Being sold."

This was an unexpected complication. The last thing he wanted was to have to find Shannon here. He had promised to help the Emperor, and there was Rory to worry about as well. But there seemed to be no way around it. He loved Shannon as much as he had ever loved anybody.

"We have to go after her."

"We will, lad, but it might not be easy."

"I'll do whatever it takes."

"Yeah, let's go," agreed Rory.

They headed out in the direction indicated. If only Shannon had had a trace on her, they could have tracked them right to his lair. On the way, Seamus Todd practiced his new shape shifting power. Elves on their second lives can transform themselves into another shape once a day. Some adepts have managed to have several forms, but it is much easier to stick with one form and practice it until it is mastered. There was nothing saying that it had to be an animal, though, only animate. It was hard, but he finally transformed into a butterfly, surprising Rory. They spent three precious days of their ten-day grace period before their search and inquiries led them along the caravan routes to a palatial estate. The kind that might belong to a sheik that could afford an elf as a slave.

"I'm going in."

"Can I come, too?" Asked Rory.

"We might need to make a sudden escape."

"I'll sit in the driver's seat and watch for you."

"Thanks. If we come out running, you might need to get us out of here in a hurry."

Seamus Todd had been practicing for days, and he now transformed into a butterfly with cobalt blue wings.

Seamus Todd the butterfly slunk silently along until he reached a window and slid in through the crack. He kept the new form while exploring the house, but finally found a locked door with bars on the window. He looked inside, but it was too dark for even an Elf to see more than a glimpse of a figure in white. He turned into a boy again and knocked softly.

"I told you if you so much as lay a finger on me, I'll cut my heart out."

"No, I don't remember you saying that at all."

"Seamus Todd? Is that you?"

"Who else would it be, traveling through the desert to save you?"

She came closer. There was no doubt it was Shannon. She was dressed in a white robe, tight around the ankles in the Eastern style, instead of wide skirted like the North, but it was definitely Shannon. He opened the door, and they were in each other's arms.

"Seamus Todd, I thought everyone had given up on me. We have to get out of here."

"We will." He took her hand and led her down the stairs to the first floor and toward the front door.

It was a princely palace they passed, he thought. Gold candelabras and silver-plated items hung among expensive paintings. Seamus Todd had no time to appreciate the kidnapper's taste.

"Stop! You're stealing my slave, eh?"

"You stole me," said Shannon.

"You stole my sister," said Seamus Todd, facing the slave master across the entrance way.

"Did you really think you could get away?"

"Of course, she's getting away, and I am going to help her. Get out of my way."

The big sheik's only answer was to launch himself at Seamus Todd. They rolled over together, the bigger demon trying to take Seamus Todd by the throat. Seamus Todd tried to stun him, but his opponent twisted the right hand out of the way, rendering it practically useless.

Seamus Todd fought back, but he was getting the air choked out of him. Just then, he felt one of his seizures coming on. The room was growing dark, stars and planets danced before his eyes. . .

There was a walloping crack and the Demon rolled away from him, falling to the floor in a heap. Shannon stood over him with a candelabra.

"Don't touch my baby brother," she snarled. She hit him again for good measure, though he was already unconscious.

An alarm rang somewhere.

"Come on, we're getting out of here."

They ran to the car. As promised, Rory was ready for them. The car was taking off before they even closed the door. The Demon sheik burst out the door after them – and turned to stone.

"We did it."

"Shannon, this is Emperor, Harsha, and Rory, a bandit."

"What have you been up to?" She asked as she bowed to the Emperor.

"It's a long story."

The slaver's estate was soon left far behind. At this rate, they should be across Asia Minor in three more days and into Greece, where they would be safe.

Their travel was interrupted the next day, though, by a sudden complication.

"Sand storm. Sand storm!"

"What'll we do?"

"Stop and wait until it blows over. There's nothing else we can do."

"Shouldn't we find shelter?"

"There isn't time."

"I thought I saw some houses over that way. We'll hurry and try to get there in time."

He drove on through the gathering darkness. In a moment, the sandstorm had caught up with them, and the little car was buried in a black gale. Visibility was reduced to the inside of the vehicle. Determined, he drove on. He knew he had seen a house straight ahead before the storm broke, and he hoped to make it there in time.

They made it. It was a white two-story stucco, with a garden around it. Nobody seemed to be home, but he knocked anyway. When no one came and the garden seemed to be overgrown, he cautiously opened the door and stepped inside.

The little house in the desert seemed to be unoccupied. The youth ran out to the car and got the others. When they got inside and slammed the door, the roaring noise was reduced to a whisper.

"Well, here we are, wherever here is."

Shannon said, "I'll see what I can find to eat."

"I'll look for weapons," said Rory.

"Weapons?" Asked Seamus Todd.

They were soon setting around the table, eating cans of beef stew and biscuits. It was a pleasant place to be, out of the howling wind and driving rain. Everyone else seemed to feel better, except the Emperor.

"Your majesty, is everything all right?"

He shook his head but declined to say what was bothering him. Seamus Todd thought it must be a combination of things. Shannon told them how she had come from Ireland to help her brother, only to be sold into slavery and need rescuing herself. Rory was in a good mood and told jokes and stories to keep every one's mood up.

"A lion grabbed a monkey and said, "who is king of the beasts?" The monkey said, "you are," so the lion let him go. He came upon a zebra and asked, who was king of the beasts? "You are, mighty king," said the zebra, so he let him go. Then he came upon an elephant and asked her, "who do you say is the king of beasts?" The elephant grabbed him with her trunk, whirled him around, and tossed him into an acacia tree. As he staggered away, he said, "if you didn't know the answer, you could have just said so."

Seamus Todd laughed harder than the joke deserved. Shannon laughed politely, but the Emperor was so wrapped in gloom he didn't even notice.

"I want a trial," he said at last.

"What kind of trial, your majesty? Of who?"

"Of me. What have I done by giving Pryadar the kingdom. I fear it will be the ruin of all I have done."

"You didn't give it to him, your majesty. He took it."

"I know, and terrible things can happen when the succession is broken. Pryadar. Have you come here for judgment?"

Seamus Todd followed the old man's gaze, but there was nothing there.

"You're imagining things, your majesty."

"My son, what have you done?"

After a while he got up and went to bed. There were several rooms, so the rest of them went to bed, too.

In the middle of the night, he went and checked on everybody. Rory was sleeping contentedly. Shannon was breathing lightly.

The Emperor was gone.

From his bedroom, and the whole house.

Seamus Todd raced out into the storm.

"Emperor, where are you?" The wind seemed to throw his words back in his face. Just then he caught a glimpse of a figure in the darkness. He was wandering around with his face covered against the ubiquitous sand.

"Your majesty, you've got to come back in."

"Please, just leave me alone."

"I'm not leaving you out here. Come inside."

"I don't deserve any better than this."

"Come inside. There are a lot of people counting on you."

"Not anymore. I may have let them down, but I'm free of the burden."

"And what about Shannon and Rory and me? We're still here. Come inside."

He finally relented and followed him back into the house.

They spent the next day and night waiting for the storm to blow out. Seamus Todd and Shannon were finally able to call home and reassure Mom that they were all right.

"Mom, we're all right."

"Seamus Todd?"

"And Shannon. We're together."

"Hi, mom," said Shannon.

"Hello," said Rory.

"Rory says hello, too."

"Who's Rory?"

"A friend we picked up along the way. The Emperor would say hi, too, but he's resting."

They explained how the Emperor had been exiled and how they had wandered together to this place in what he believed was Asia Minor. He made sure to mention Pryadar's treachery and faithlessness, very different from the way Elves treat one another.

"Pryadar is a monster," he finished.

"I know, dear, that was why I was reluctant to let you go. You have such a good sweet heart, you're no match for Pryadar."

"Well, I always thought love was a match for hate. Surely, if I love as much as he hates, things are even?"

"I don't know, sweetie. But hurry home soon. We're all waiting for you."

That night, a cry in the darkness.

"My boy!"

Seamus Todd was awake and down the hallway in a moment. "Yes, I'm right here."

"I think it's time."

"Time for what? It's the middle of the night. Oh. No. You can't go."

"I'm already dying, my boy, and you can't prevent it."

Rory raced in, then, and he asked him to get Shannon. She was always the nurse in their little family. She came at once, her diaphanous gown wrinkled.

She examined him. "I'm sorry, Seamus Todd, there's nothing we can do."

"What if we got him to a doctor?"

"Seamus Todd, he's an old, old man. He shouldn't have been out here in the first place. You did everything you could."

"He's dying?"

"I'm sorry."

"I thought we would have longer."

They kept a vigil about his bed. By three, he was in a coma.

By dawn, the storm blew itself out. The Emperor was dead.

The man who ruled three realms for most of his life was buried in a country garden, with a few flowers to mark it. By unspoken agreement, there was no tombstone. Seamus Todd was afraid Pryadar would dig it up to prove his father was dead or subject the corpse to other indignities. The old man had suffered enough in his life, they didn't need to add more to it by being indecorous on his grave.

Naganandini sat at her vanity, combing her hair as her husband approached.

"Hello, darling. How do you like your new bracelet? Still shy? Don't worry about it, it looks lovely."

Jason said nothing.

"It's a slave bracelet, dear. It robs you of all conscious thought. Running the country is so much easier when there's only one person to do it, don't you agree? I thought you would."

She put down her brush and started applying her makeup.

"I have decided to continue the war against my father. Do you have any objections? I thought not. So, let's go ahead."

Jason said nothing.

"And in case we lose, I have decided to have your parents killed. Is that all right with you?"

Jason said nothing.

"I thought you'd say that."

CHAPTER EIGHT
A New Dawn

One old man short, they headed out that afternoon. They were a quiet group, including the usually talkative Rory. The Emperor was dead. Seamus Todd began to feel better as they drove on, though. They were a trio of teenagers now, heading for a homecoming with nothing to slow them down.

They stopped at the next village and were in for a surprise. An Elf came out to meet them.

"There are Elves living in the Regime?" Asked Seamus Todd.

"Yes, my child. We're less than one percent of the population, but we're here. And loyal to the Emperor, bless him."

"I'm sorry to tell you, but the Emperor passed away. Yesterday."

"How terrible, we've heard nothing."

"Yes," said Seamus Todd, "and that makes Pryadar Emperor."

"You might not want to stay here now that he's the Emperor. He hates Elves," said Shannon.

That was news to Seamus Todd, but he didn't say anything.

"I know he's no Harsha, but where would we go?"

"How about to Tuatha?"

"Yeah, with the rest of the Elves," said Rory.

"Come with me, you'd better speak to the mayor."

Shortly after, they were shown into a lovely living room with several of the town's most prominent citizens. The mayor's wife served tea and cookies, and they discussed the Emperor's death and how it might affect the citizens.

"His passing was peaceful," Seamus Todd assured them. "Now I think we might have to worry about what will happen next."

There was a knock on the door.

"Is the mayor here?"

"Yes."

"Soldiers from the Regime are asking for you."

A Genie general or something like that stormed into the room, scowled at them and said, "all the able-bodied male Elves are to assemble peacefully in the town square by noon to be inducted into the army. All the women and children and all the little Elves too little to fight will join the back of the train. Hurry up."

"And if we resist?"

"The city will be burned to the ground with all its people still in it. You have until noon."

The general walked out.

"You heard him, get everyone into the city square as soon as possible."

"You're not going to surrender just like that, are you?"

"Of course not. We're going to fight," said the Mayor. "We need to get organized."

Armed Elves were gathering in the streets. Seamus Todd was discouraged to note they not only looked defeated, but most of them didn't have sufficient weapons. Enough guns might have made a difference, but they were mostly wielding swords and other, more honorable weapons. They would be cut down like flies in the face of the enemy's lasers and advanced weaponry.

"They're going to get killed," agreed Shannon when he pointed it out.

"I don't see how Elves can be so loyal to the Regime in the first place," said Rory. "This is going to be a disaster."

"I think we should try to run," said Seamus Todd. "We're outnumbered and outgunned."

The three teenagers and various other Elves were sent from house to house in order to prepare everyone. If they weren't warriors, if they were women, children, Gnomes, Sylphs, Dwarves, Fairies or Brownies, Seamus Todd told them to start running.

The attack began before the eleventh hour was over. Apparently, the army was in a hurry. The Elves gathered around the fountain were only about a hundred warriors, besides Pixies, Fairies, and other noncombatants.

The enemy army fired gigantic nets over and into the crowd. Seamus Todd and his crew dashed out into the battle to try to help them. As he slashed at the netting, he told Rory, "at least they're still interested in taking prisoners."

"That's not what they're for," replied Rory. He didn't elaborate.

"At least you're here." He meant that he was helping the Elves in a noble cause, instead of his own people.

"Yeah, well." And he winked.

Flaming weapons were being used, and the houses around them started to burn. Soon, they would be surrounded by flames.

The General, if that was what he was, appeared, facing the crowd. His troops of Genies came swarming around him, and the battle began in earnest. The fighting and smoke made everything a confused mass of whirling bodies, dust and shrapnel. Seamus Todd joined in the fighting. His laser cut down enemies right and left. If they had had more, it would have made a big difference, but it had come mostly down to swords and guns, and both sides were equally matched for the moment. There were about the same numbers of fighters on each side. Pryadar's forces couldn't drive their tanks through the barricades, though they would soon have them down. And then they would even roll right over their own troops to destroy the enemy.

And then Rory was running straight at the general, his arms raised in surrender -

"Oh, no," Seamus Todd gasped at the sudden betrayal -

And the general raised a sword to kill the boy.

And Rory pulled a small gun he'd taken from a dying soldier and shot the General.

For a moment, the fighting almost stopped on both sides as everyone stood aghast. Then it resumed more fiercely than ever.

So Rory wasn't a traitor after all. He dashed back to the Elven side and smashed into Seamus Todd. They embraced in the middle of battle. Then they had to get back to work, because the enemy was pressing into them.

"I was hoping if they lost their general they'd give up the fight," he explained.

"Sorry, it didn't work."

The battle continued. The Elves were trying to reform their lines and move their dead and wounded out of the way. The Elves with lasers were turning the tide of battle, and there were more Regime soldiers dying than Elves, but it couldn't last. Seamus Todd knew that soon enough the enemy laser squad would devastate the rebels. And there would be far more enemy lasers, as well as other weaponry.

He was close to the mayor when he saw him fall with a horrifying gash on his side. He ran to him and caught him as he fell.

"Sir, we have to retreat."

"Give the order. . ."

It was his last words. Seamus Todd felt his life draining from the man's body with his blood. He got blood all over his shirt and right hand.

He grabbed a banner lying half broken on the ground and waved the Elves toward the north and escape. "Come on, everyone."

Buildings on both sides of the street were burning as they retreated. Fire and smoke were blinding and choking, but they continued to fight the foe in an orderly retreat.

The Genies also fell back, exhausted. But they would regroup, and in far greater numbers. They had to get away.

Seamus Todd found himself the leader of a group of exiles. He bore the black and orange standard of the Regime to try to convince their pursuers that they were a group of loyal supporters. Shannon took over driving the car, filling it full of refugees. A bunch of other cars winded slowly behind them. Together, they passed through Asia Minor.

It was a more mountainous terrain than the river valley. It wasn't an unattractive place, but Seamus Todd wanted to get through it as quickly as possible and reach the golden horn, where they would pass the Regime's border. Then they would be in Greece, which, he knew gave amnesty to all those seeking to escape the Regime.

He looked back to see the burning village. It seemed like such a waste. Elves could be completely loyal to the empire of their enemy, and he didn't care. They had served the Emperor for years and might have made excellent soldiers for his cause.

Instead, he turned them against him. Poor Pryadar had no idea what he had done.

"What's that?"

"The invading army. We're behind them."

He hadn't forgotten the invasion force, he'd just had more pressing problems. He was hoping there might be some way around them, or they could escape detection, but of course that now seemed absurd. The more intelligent commanders of the army would be at the back, not the mindless ghouls. They had bumped into the rear of the army heading toward Tuatha.

They pushed on anyway, unable to do anything else. They couldn't stay here forever, and they couldn't turn back. They were in trouble again.

"Well, there's no way they can escape us now," he quipped.

"Maybe we can try disguising ourselves."

"And waltz up right behind them? What are we going to do if it doesn't work?"

"I don't know."

They came to the Bosporus, where the Regime had built a bridge. On the other side was Europe – and safety. Trouble was, the tail end of the invasion force was still using it. Seamus Todd signaled everyone else to stay behind and went up to the commander in charge like he owned the place.

"I'm Seamus Todd McKenzie, aka Prince Ravana. I'm bringing the contingent of Elves from the village of Sramralla to join the army. Sorry we're late."

"Prince Ravana."

"That's what I said."

"I heard he died."

"He did. I was chosen to take his place."

"You're an Elf."

"My whole group is Elves. Do you think they can't be as loyal to the new Emperor as they were to the old?"

"No, I don't. Lord Pryadar has ordered death or slavery for every Elf in the nation."

"And do you agree with his insane demands?"

"Yes, I do."

"Why do you hate Elves?"

"They're a burden on our just society, parasites. They should be killed like so many other parasites have been wiped out."

"Pryadar can't think that." For all his flaws, his near insanity, and his grandiosity, Pryadar had never shown any sign of being a bigot. He didn't hate Seamus Todd for being an Elf. Why was he defending him?

"Well, we're joining the army and you can't stop us."

"I'm not going to. Go out there and get yourself killed. The sooner the better."

"Thank you." With a sigh of relief, he rejoined his followers and they started across the bridge. Technically, they couldn't be attacked after they left the Regime, but Pryadar's supporters weren't much for technicalities.

Just then, the pursuing army appeared over the next hill. They were closing in, fast.

"Get across the bridge," he yelled.

The whole group started running as fast as they could while still tightly packed together.

The front of Seamus Todd's group came screeching to a halt just behind the body of the main army.

The back of the army contained mostly bearers and other lowlifes, but there were several tanks in sight and a command vehicle.

Things were looking bad. He had tried to lead them to safety, and unwittingly walked into a trap. The Genies were bringing their weapons to bear.

"Halt."

A figure was trying to force his way through the melee. The confused Genies lowered their weapons.

"Rustem?"

"Seamus Todd?"

They met and embraced. Rustem turned gold with joy. The Genies and the Elves stopped fighting each other.

"These Elves are under my protection. They will accompany us into Greece and follow us into the Elven realm."

"Thanks, Rustem."

The refugees marched on proudly, leaving the three of them in the car alone again.

They went into the city with seven names, which had included Byzantium and Istanbul. They were looking for the embassy, so they could get word to their parents. They were told to go across the street to a restaurant and await instructions. So, they did. The waiter came up to them and announced a visitor.

"Presenting, a file clerk from the fifth army."

"Dad? Dad?"

Shannon joined them in a group hug.

"Let me look at you. My poor boy," he said, brushing the hair away from his bandages. "We can get that fixed, you know."

"Dad, this is Rory. He's been helping us all this time."

"A pleasure to meet you, my boy."

"And Prince Rustem."

The five of them had dinner at the restaurant overlooking the bay.

"We talked to Mom, and she and Siobhan are doing fine."

"Good."

"But I promised I'd go back."

"But you mustn't."

"I told Aliyah she could come with me. I'd be breaking my promise."

"Would she keep her promise if the situation was reversed?"

"I don't know, but it doesn't matter. I promised."

"What is there to go back to?" Asked Shannon.

"There's revenge."

"On Pryadar."

"He's not worth it."

"He's the most powerful man on earth and he's not worth it? He has to be stopped."

"You're not the one to do it."

His father said, "Seamus Todd, you're a child of love, not hate. The first word you said was love. You were a day old."

"It was?"

"I was there. We have it recorded."

"You said "love" clearly," Shannon said.

"Well that's nice, but I don't see what that has to do with anything."

"No, you shouldn't go back," said Rustem. "My dad will only find ways to hurt you. He wouldn't keep his word if it was him."

"But he's a liar. I'm not."

"Doesn't anyone support me?"

"No."

"No."

"No."

"No."

The main course came, a roast boar.

"All right, then."

"I want you to promise me."

"To promise is to lie."

He looked up to see them all staring at him.

"I'm sorry, it happened again." His epilepsy was acting up again.

"We'd better take you to the hotel and get some rest soon."

"As soon as dinner is finished," he agreed. With a smile.

Early the next morning before anyone else was up, Seamus Todd slipped out of the boy's room and scurried down the stairs. Rustem was waiting for him by the car.

"Please don't stop me."

"I'm coming with you."

They were in the car and on his way before those in the hotel realized he was gone. There was a letter on his bed.

Dear Dad,

I'm sorry I have to do this. Please return home safely, I'll be back as soon as I can. I made a promise and I have to keep my promises. Please, take Rory along, as he doesn't have any family. I love you all. That's why I have to do this.

Seamus Todd

It took him several days to drive back, and his timing couldn't have been worse. He was in the city, carefully driving along, when he saw the flash of light. In a moment, the whole earth seemed to shudder. Dark smoke was rising in the distance. He hurried to the tower, where everyone else was converging at the same time.

If it was a laser blast, as he was guessing it was, it meant the Regime army was at the border of Tuatha. Since the hostages had been freed, the Elves had a free hand, and had struck at the capital.

The tower had been split open by a laser from an Elven satellite. The head of the sphinx had fallen off and rolled away. The curtain tore, and the face was revealed. It looked like Seamus Todd's face. As he had looked before Alexis. Now, it was cracked just like where his face was scarred.

The tower looked like lightning struck it. In addition to the head being sheared off, the wings lay broken on the ground and the entire structure was pouring black smoke out of every nook and cranny. Its heating system exploded, adding to the damage with a series of smaller implosions and explosions. People were running out of the single large door like a kicked ants hill. Some were screaming, adding to the chaos of noise.

Even as he watched, the rest of the building shuddered under another blow, and the structure split from crown to base. Like the shriek of a dying man, the building collapsed in on itself, making the ground rumble and throwing up a great cloud of dust and smoke. Seamus Todd had never seen anything like it.

He was one of several people who dashed toward the disaster area, trying to help. People who emerged looked like ghosts, covered in ashes. He thought he recognized one of them and ran to help her first.

"Aliyah."

"Seamus Todd? You came back. I thought you were dead."

"I thought you were all dead."

"Give us time."

"That's the one thing we just ran out of."

"Are you all right?"

"Yes, but it's not fair," said Aliyah.

"What's not fair."

"Pryadar wasn't home."

Together with hundreds of other people, they started helping with the evacuation and triage. The flow of people coming from the tower slowed to a trickle, and then stopped altogether. Though the number dead, it would turn out, was relatively small, there were many injuries. Among those killed was Queen Hagar Semiramis, Pryadar's wife. Seamus Todd found her barely recognizable remains in the ruins below where the harem had been. She and several of the women had died together, in each other's arms.

Hours passed as the rescue carried on, and night fell. Finally, the triage ended, and many were brought to hospitals all over the world. Relieved, he made his way to a tent set up and fell into an exhausted slumber.

The next morning, he was up at dawn and part of the rescue team once more.

One of the Demons pointed at him and said, "this is all the fault of the Elves. Let's get him."

"No," Aliyah said. "He's on our side, he's done everything to help us through this disaster. Leave him alone."

"It's Elves like him that attacked us."

Seamus Todd felt a flash of rage, though he tried to hide it. The Asuras had started the war long ago, and the Elves were just trying to survive. The fact that they were capable of protecting themselves had never sat well with their opponents. The Regime had started the latest phase of the war, and the Elves had responded.

"I'm here to try to help."

"Kill him."

"I'm a representative to the Elves, all right? I'm here to help. Nobody else should have to die today because of this foolishness."

"You hold your tongue, demon, or I'll have you locked up," said Aliyah.

The Demon looked a little pale. Regime prisons were not playgrounds. Finally, he said "if he wants to prove himself, maybe he could help them get the people in the lower layers out."

"I'd be glad to."

Heavy equipment had been brought in, and the elevator shaft had been found that went down into the lower reaches of the building. Seamus Todd was one of the volunteers to go down and rescue the prisoners.

The base of the tower had been made to withstand attacks, so the building hadn't collapsed into the basements. With people working at lowering them on ropes and bringing up the survivors, Seamus Todd was one of the ones descending into the earth. Aliyah stayed topside, directing the rescue efforts.

With a key in one hand and a crowbar in the other, Seamus Todd set about opening the prison doors and letting out people who thought they would never again see the light of day. They emerged, blinking, into a clear morning. Both guards and prisoners, as well as various servitors, followed them up the life lines to freedom.

"Will you look who's here?" Said Aliyah, as he brought another group to safety.

"The Globe," he said. "Michael Desmond!"

So it was. Michael, Brandon and Erin showed up to offer support and help, especially with moving the wounded to various hospitals around the city.

Finally, Seamus Todd brought the last prisoner out of the deepest, darkest cell. A blind man, he came up to the cheers of the crowd. He had been without light for years. Seamus Todd hoped they would be able to do something for him. Most kinds of blindness were curable.

People cheered as the last survivor was helped to an ambulance. They made sure, but there were no more people, living or dead, in the rubble by that time.

Erin and Brandon showed up, hugged him, and brought him aboard the Globe. Rustem was there beside him.

Michael was in his office. They all trooped in together and he showed them a simulator with a glowing blue and green Earth floating in space.

"The Emperor has his counterattack all laid out. They've managed to build a fusion device."

"Then what do they need to attack us for? Why can't they leave us alone?"

"Yesterday, the ghoul army reached the border of Tuatha. Now, he'll launch his fusion powered space ship at the capital."

"The fusion reactors will destroy one another?" Seamus Todd guessed.

A tiny spaceship maneuvered its way across the globe and hit the bright spot marking Caer Wydr. A mushroom shaped cloud loomed.

"And the Elves with it."

"That's the least bad scenario. An explosion like that could tear the Earth's crust all the way to the mantle and set off a geothermic event. We'll be lucky if it doesn't destroy the entire planet, as well."

"We'll launch our own missiles."

"It won't do any good."

"What good would it do him to do this? He wants to rule the world, not destroy it."

"If he can't rule it, he may settle for destroying it. He knows how hard it will be to conquer the Elves, which was his dream. And we would keep coming back to life, except if we are all wiped out at the same time."

"You see, you have to have Elves in the world to bring the dead back. The more Elves there are, the easier it is. The fewer, the harder."

"And death by radiation, we wouldn't want to come back in forms that might be grossly mutated."

"Can we stop him?"

"We'll have to sneak aboard the launch site and steal the ship," Michael said. "Erin will lead the mission and Brandon will go along."

"It won't be easy."

"We'll find a way."

"I want to help," said Seamus Todd.

"You're just a boy."

"I'm the one that's been here, doing everything. I can help you."

"You'll have to follow orders exactly."

"All right. I want to see things through to the end. I can drive an imperial ship. Can any of you do that?" Asked Seamus Todd.

"Yes," said Brandon and Erin together.

"I represent the royal family."

"All right," said Michael. "We started this together, we will finish it together."

"Can I go along, too?" Asked Rustem. "Just to the gate. I want to make sure you're okay, but I can't stop my father."

Early the next evening, they were sneaking onto the Regime's space base in Tikrit, the Regime. Brandon was in the lead, Erin in the middle, and Seamus Todd brought up the rear, carrying the equipment. Rustem, as agreed, stayed at the gate to watch for pursuit.

The spaceship lurked on the launch pad like a giant insect. The final check was being made before the crew entered. If they were going to go, the time was now.

They dashed from building to building, ever closer. Finally, the braced themselves for the final distance. Laser guns drawn, they threw themselves up the gang plank and into the maw of the craft. Strangely, no one seemed to notice their intrusion.

The thought came into his mind as the gates shut. "It's a trap," he warned.

"Hush," warned Erin.

Neither she nor Brandon seemed overly concerned. Perhaps they were expecting it all along. Was that why they hadn't wanted him to come? It was a suicide mission.

The cockpit. Brandon slid into the seat and began the automatic check. Erin signaled him to take the left and she would take the right. They searched the ship for life forms. There didn't seem. . .

"I picked up something," he looked at his scanner. "Erin, I think you're about to encounter someone."

There was a scream, perhaps a banshee one, and Seamus Todd ran to her side to help. There was no one there in the corridor where the two dots had met, but the door was just sliding closed. Two dots were headed back toward the stern of the vessel. Brandon and Erin.

His watch clicked. "Abort mission." The bodyguard and the protegee diplomat scrambled out the door before it closed.

"Where's Seamus Todd?" Asked Brandon.

"He didn't get off."

Seamus Todd froze, uncertain what to do. While he hesitated, he felt the ship rise and lift off. They were launched. A two-hundred-ton missile with a fusion reactor warhead was on its way like the fourth horseman of the apocalypse. The desert of Mesopotamia fell away behind them, and its long graceful arc aimed it toward Northern Europe.

He burst into the bridge, where a figure sat at the controls. Someone with a blocky head as though carved out of granite and covered in what looked like moss. The Poid.

He turned toward him, seeming genuinely surprised, if not alarmed. He pulled out a gun and motioned the boy to come in.

"Seamus Todd McKenzie."

"What are you doing here?"

"Fulfilling my mission. Especially, to make sure the Elves were defeated. Now our mission is complete. I am the one chosen to drive the ship into the capital. My name will be written on the scroll of martyrs."

"I don't feel like joining you."

"Then you shouldn't have come aboard. Too late to stop me now. Look."

Seamus Todd saw the view screen showing hundreds of ships falling in line behind them. "Our ships full of everyone who is supposed to survive will watch from a distance to kill any survivors. We'll rule what's left of the planet."

"Assuming there's anything left. What about you?"

"I will live forever as the hero who destroyed the Elves and ended the Perpetual War."

"You'll die."

"What price glory?"

"I'll stop you."

"Do you think you can? You're nothing but a whelp of a boy."

Seamus Todd backed up under the unpitying glare of the weapon, into the artificial gravity machine. He came to a sudden decision and turned and shut off the machine.

"What are you doing?"

Seamus Todd, the Poid, and various objects floated off the floor and into the air. The Poid launched himself at the boy, who was bringing up his gauntlet. They met in the middle of the cabin, as Asia Minor rolled beneath them. Greece and Italy were coming up on the window screen.

The gun met the gauntlet, and the blow knocked them apart in the zero gravity. They bounced back to their respective corners and started at each other again.

For what seemed like several minutes but was probably only seconds they fought. Seamus Todd was dueling left handed because he hoped to stun his foe without hurting him. It was a hard fight, though. The Poid was bigger and stronger than he was.

He managed to get a blow on the Poid's rock-like skin. He froze and started to drift aimlessly. Seamus Todd managed to turn the gravity back on, and he and the Poid fell. For a moment he lay on the deck floor, crushed by his battle with a tough foe. He closed his eyes and hoped the epilepsy would kick in again, so he would not know what happened when he died.

Get up, Seamus Todd.

"No, I'm beaten," he thought, exhausted. "Get someone else to save the world."

There is no one else. I will help you. Get up.

He sat up and saw out the window. An eagle. It had to be a hallucination. No real eagle was that big, that fast, or survived so high. But it looked at him with fierce love in its eyes, and he staggered to his feet.

Seamus Todd rushed to the pilot's chair and managed to buckle himself in. Trying to learn to fly a spaceship while it was hurtling through the atmosphere was not the easiest way to go about it, but he knew how to fly a spaceship from his practicing in games. He followed the eagle, which was now leading the spaceship. He began to push up.

The Miracle Mountains were hurtling by. Tuatha was right below them. And still they climbed. They were gaining altitude. Too slowly.

He grabbed the radio.

"My lord, Pryadar's new aide got his attention. We're receiving a transmission from the spaceship."

"Onscreen." A fuzzy image filled the hologram portal.

"This is Seamus Todd McKenzie. I am here."

"No," said Pryadar.

The boy just had time to realize he was seeing the North and Baltic seas with the jutting peninsula between them, and then the soaring crystal towers were in sight. He struggled to change the ship's course. It was like bending metal, getting the control to turn.

Follow the eagle, he thought.

Closer, closer. . .

His teeth were gritted, his face pale.

"You're too late," said the Poid.

The ship soared above the pinnacles of the castle of crystal by about three feet. They clipped a flagpole and it went spinning toward the earth, flag and all.

"No!" It was the Poid again. He was stunned but apparently his mouth still worked.

Seamus Todd collapsed across the controls with relief.

"You fool. It's rigged to explode."

"What?"

"I said . . ."

"I heard you. Don't you realize it might take out the fleet, as well?"

"What do I care?"

Seamus Todd grabbed the controls and pushed upward with all his might. The eagle looked back and nodded.

They were climbing up, almost vertically into a dark sky. The following armada fell back, with the Elven fleet pursuing the Asura ships as they broke away.

"We have to get out of here."

"My time is up," said the Poid.

He looked back to see his adversary floating in midair. He had turned off the gravity again, but Seamus Todd was wearing his seatbelt. When he looked back the eagle broke away.

Well done. It seemed to crackle into lightning, and it was gone.

For a moment, Seamus Todd seriously considered leaving him. But he had stunned him, so he was responsible for what happened to him. He ran to get him, dragging him down the corridor toward the exit.

The Poid was beginning to get his strength back. He fought. Realizing he would actually get himself killed and take himself with him, he pushed him toward the airlock. He pulled open the window, and the wind came screaming in around them.

"You're not going to kill me?"

"We'll escape together, I'll carry. . ."

He never got to finish what he was going to say. The alien slapped him across the face, Seamus Todd let go and there was a scream and he was gone. They were over the ocean, and he knew it was fatal to Poids. They sank.

He jumped out the window, tearing off his cloak to use his wings. He just got them spread when he felt the burst of heat above him. He fell like Icarus, flapping wildly in the hope of at least slowing his descent.

Then the sound wave struck him, and he lost consciousness. So, he was one of the few who didn't see what happened next.

The people of Caer Wydr, awakened by the near miss, were already out in the streets, watching the spaceships fly past. Then the ship's reactor exploded, and the lights of the ships faded out, and the stars fled, and the night became brighter than day.

Naganandini, having been alerted by the sounds, ran out on the balcony as the new day star appeared. She watched in shocked awe as she realized how close her father had come to taking her life and the lives of everyone around her.

Caroline and Siobhan heard the noise and came running out of the lighthouse. Side by side they watched as the wreckage of the ship ascended, floating higher and higher. Then it bloomed like a rose, and the cloud of smoke cleared away to reveal the birth of the new god, the sun.

Their hands came together, and they watched silently. It was a new day. The shadows grew black and sharp as knife blades.

"It's Seamus Todd's star," said his older sister. It was a guess, but she guessed right. It would be forever known as Seamus Todd's star.

"I know. I just don't know if he's all right."

"Do you know what this means?"

"The capital is safe?"

"That, too. But it means that night didn't follow day."

"And day didn't follow night."

Erin, Brandon and Rustem, watched as the new sun rose in the west.

"I think the capital is safe," said Erin. "I'll call to make sure."

"Seamus Todd did it," said Rustem. "Yes!"

Brandon just smiled.

On the border of Tuatha, a battle was blazing. The exhausted Elves were falling back, overwhelmed by numbers. Even though they had laser guns, traps, and courage, they were simply exhausted. The zombie hordes had died by the thousands, but there were still four billion or more left.

And then the nova, the new star was born. The black cloud covering them was ripped apart by the hot winds, and sunlight fell on them. The ghouls had just enough time to look up and feel the warmth on their decaying skin, and then they fell.

All four billion of them. The demons froze in their legions, never to move again on their own. They had become hard as stone.

As the Elves scrambled to their feet, the zombies melted, their faces contorting, their flesh shriveling, a ghastly sweet stench of death rose in billowing clouds, and then it was over. All that was left of the greatest army the world had ever known was a pile of decaying bones and ashes. The front line had passed two meters into Tuatha.

Thousands of miles away, the rest of the army ground to a halt. Looking at the splinters of their former army lying there, they realized they were far from the front line, and no longer a match for the army of Tuatha. The tanks, ships soldiers and all their combined might was little without the army of the undead.

Pryadar watched from remote view from the air base. He saw his majestic fleet trailing the lead ship, saw them veering off as the capital approached. He saw the ship barely miss the crystal castle and go flying off over the Atlantic. Then the ship exploded, and he lost his feed.

He didn't overreact. His jaw clenched.

Finally, he smiled. And his entourage stepped back in terror.

Beads of sweat trickled down his three faces from his hairlines to his jaws, leaving a faint stream. Still, he said nothing. The next person to speak would have his head taken off. Seconds ticked by. They waited for him to yell, scream, throw things, or sentence them all to death. Instead, he turned on his heel and walked out of the room.

There was silence behind him.

The birds, confused, awoke and began to sing. Insects buzzed, and flowers opened, as all nature reacted to the new light.

Poids

The original Poid War lasted ten years, and the first Alien contact was the beginning of the Fifth Age. After tremendous losses, the Poids surrendered. A handful of the Aliens remained on Earth to advise the Asuras and seek the downfall of the Elves. Their reproductive habits and society are carefully concealed secrets. Only one Poid was left at the end of the Perpetual War, and he died in 5525 while falling from the fusion ship. He hit the Atlantic and sank like a stone.

CHAPTER NINE

Space War

Cold.

Cold and dark.

The cold bit into his bones, gnawing at him.

He tried to move. His arm seemed to float away. He realized he was floating in an icy sea. He gasped, filling his lungs.

He tried to sit up and look around, almost sank. Chunks of ice filled the water around him. The sun was almost overhead, but it didn't warm him. He realized he was in danger of hypothermia. He turned on his stomach and tried to paddle. It was swimming through thick liquid, his limbs hung heavy and frozen.

He was hoping moving would make him warmer, but it was useless. All it did was drain his energy. He was going to die, and sink into the endless abyss, where he couldn't be found and rescued. The thought distressed him less than it might have. He was so very cold, and all he wanted to do was rest.

But a large piece of ice wasn't far away, and it was smooth and flat. He figured he could swim to it and they could at least find his body. His family would feel better about it.

He climbed on and shook himself. It was almost a futile gesture, but at least it kept him warm. The sun was still up, so it had to be Aquarius First. His birthday.

Almost every step threatened to break the ice, so he finally huddled down. The wind wasn't fierce, but it was more than enough to steal his precious body heat. Soon, he was shivering uncontrollably. He waited for either rescue or death. It was a very pretty place he had chosen to die, and Elves withstood cold better than heat, but he knew he probably had less than an hour. He considered walking back into the water to die but decided not to. If death was coming for him, let it work to get him. He had already met it halfway.

Seamus Todd tried stretching his wings to get them dry. They weren't scaled and bright but feathered. He had metamorphosed again. Which meant he had died again. . .

Seamus Todd looked up; sure he wouldn't see a ship on the horizon. So, he was more than a little surprised that one was there. Surely, he was hallucinating? It grew and grew, and soon there could be no doubt. It was a ship. He stood up as best he was able and waved to them.

In a moment the rescue boat had him aboard, stripping him out of his wet clothes, shoveling chicken noodle soup and cocoa down his throat. It was ht, but he didn't complain. He was safe again.

When he was dressed and rested a little, the captain came and hugged him. "I'm so glad we found you. You saved the capital, lad. Good job."

"And where are we now?" He asked.

"Off Greenland. In the middle of nowhere. Trying to find you was like trying to find a needle in a haystack, but we did it. We figured where you might have fallen. Now, the king would like to talk to you."

"The king?"

"King emeritus, I mean. King Blake. Jason and Naganandini are still king and queen."

"For now, anyway," said a seaman under his breath.

"Is something wrong in Denmark?"

"Impeachment proceedings have started against them, but I'll explain all that later. King Blake. Your majesty," he said as the former king appeared in the view screen.

"Seamus Todd, I'm glad to see you're safe."

"Grandfather, you too."

"Have you grown a little, lad?"

"I think I have."

"The Zombie army was defeated when you unleashed the new sun. Since night didn't follow day, we've declared this the dawn of a new age, the Sixth Age of Man. The double long day will be remembered by the Elves forever. This is Aquarius First, the first day of the New Age. Thanks to you."

"And your leadership."

"I can't take any credit. It's all yours. The government will be contacting the Regime later today and start negotiating a ceasefire. Hopefully, the new age will be more peaceful than the last."

"Happy New Year," said Seamus Todd.

"Happy birthday."

"The Globe is coming to pick you up."

"Thank you."

They continued back to Europe, with the Globe growing larger in the distance. Finally, the two ships met, and Seamus Todd was taken aboard.

He had expected Michael Desmond and his crew, Erin and Brandon and maybe Rustem. He was surprised but overjoyed to find his whole posse was there. Dad, Shannon, Rory, and Aliyah were all there.

"You've grown, haven't you."

"He sure seems to have."

"Will you be an angel or a giant?"

Dad looked thoughtful. "Maybe you're both."

"You mean. . ."

"One out of every million transformations, there's a mutation, and the result is a seraph."

"I'm a seraph?" His eyes seemed to glow. "Does that mean. . ."

Just then, Michael burst in and hugged him. "I'm glad you're all right," he said.

"You, too."

"If we could discuss the new star for a moment. . ."

"Yes."

"Right now, the new star is in geosynchronous orbit, so there is no night on Earth. The new star continues to draw further and further away from us. Soon it will be beyond Mars, and then Jupiter, and finally it will leave our solar system all together. So, night and day will resume after about three days."

"Good."

"I wanted you to hear this," said Michael. He brought up a disc and slid it in the player. "The transmitter you placed in Pryadar's gun picked this up this morning."

Pryadar's voice: "Can we have the fleet ready to go in a days' time?"

A. "Yes, your majesty, but our armada is no match for the Elvish defense force."

"That wasn't what I asked." He didn't sound angry. "I asked if we could be ready to go, admiral."

Admiral: "Yes, your majesty. I can have most of the armada ready by Friday. There are some ships still being repaired, but I can get ten warships with a hundred interceptors and support craft in the air."

"That will do."

"Your majesty, permission to speak freely."

"You may."

"They'll cut us to pieces."

"I know. It doesn't matter. We've already lost. Admiral."

"Yes, sir?"

"If you have a chance to reach the capital, and I'm not saying you will, try to spare my daughter."

"Of course, your majesty."

The tape continued, setting out details, but Seamus Todd got the main idea. "They're planning another attack."

"And we're going to have to be ready to meet him in the air."

"But we can beat them now, can't we? Our fleet is more than twice as big as theirs."

"Four times bigger. But it will involve a costly battle and suffering. The war isn't over yet."

"But it's their last gasp."

"We want you to lead the defense. You'll be in the flagship."

"Me?"

"It's merely an honorary position. You're the hero of the Elves, and we want everyone to know who's responsible for our victory."

Like his being a translator for the mission. Yes, he could do that.

They landed in Paris the next day, and in the morning, the entire fleet assembled in preparation for the final battle. With the rest of them, he raised his right hand and took the oath of a Tuathan soldier.

"I pledge allegiance to the kingdom of Tuatha.
I will be loyal to our king and queen.

I will not leave a fellow soldier behind.
I will support the cause of Elves everywhere.
I will not harm a prisoner of war."

An Elven general addressed them. "Remember, if you drift off into space, you won't revive. We have to be connected to the Earth, or at least in the atmosphere around it. Your lives, and the lives of everyone in the battle, is important."

They scattered to their ships and prepared for take-off. There were twenty-five battle ships, long and slim, whose energy wings unfolded like a butterfly's. Seamus Todd's ship was the Io. Twenty Polyphemus class carriers. Over four hundred slim, glass bubbled interceptors were prepared, some aboard the carriers, others would be free ranging. Spiky skippers, fierce dragonfly shaped fighters. The whole group was electrified with excitement. They weren't just going to defend their kingdom, they were going to take the war to the Regime. After the space battle, they were going to go on to defeat what was left of the Regime's army. The enemy was going to fight hard, but they were going to lose. The war was only going to last a few more days before they sued for peace.

The engines roared to life, and they were lifting off. Paris fell away beneath them, and the Miracle Mountains loomed ahead. And the other ships appeared, like mosquitoes, like flies, like eagles and finally the armada of the Regime, weapons firing. The two sides met like thunderclouds along the border. Battle was joined.

Laser cannons from the Elven defense base began firing as soon as they were in range, and the Regime ships were soon jarred out of formation. The Tuathan ships swept in and dogfights broke out.

The Io was not only a battle ship. It was a hospital ship, capable of linking to any ship on either side and rescuing the crew. It was a heavy responsibility, because the Asura ships weren't designed with either safety or comfort. Most pilots and crew headed out with the prospect they were never coming back. The job of the crew aboard the Io was to rescue as many brave fighters as they could. Smaller ships could be brought aboard the landing dock with tractor beams. Larger ships could be connected, and their crews brought on board.

There was soon work to do. The Io captured a small interceptor ship and its crew. Seamus Todd welcomed them aboard.

"Go ahead and kill us," snarled the captain.

"Kill you? Who wants to kill you?"

"The Elves. We know what happens to prisoners."

"You'll be taken to Paris to await extradition. You're going home."

"Elves torture and kill their prisoners."

"Who told you that? We took an oath not to harm prisoners we captured."

"The Regime told us that. Lord Alexis told us that. That's why we were willing to fight to the death."

"Is that the first and only time the Regime has ever lied to you? When did Alexis do anything but lie? Don't worry. You're safe."

"I think you're just playing with us."

He finally convinced the prisoners they would come to no harm. They trooped into a comfortable cell.

They captured seven enemy ships and three allied ones. Each of the enemy soldiers had to be reassured they weren't going to be tortured. Seamus Todd had to explain it all over again, the Elves were simply glad to be rescued. The battle was fierce, but the Elves were winning.

The Emperor's flagship, the Gargantua, largest ship on either side, was aflame. Rather than letting the Io approach, it made a suicidal dash at the nearest city on the mountain. Three ships pursued it, and it fell flaming out of the sky.

Seamus Todd bowed his head in acknowledgment of a gallant foe.

They were too late to save the Gargantua, but the Io quickly captured a small interceptor.

"Lord McKenzie," said an aide. "The prisoner asked for you. Specifically."

"Me?"

"By name. It's the Emperor."

"The Emperor."

"Seamus Todd, are you all right?"

"Excuse me, I have to make a phone call."

All kinds of ideas started percolating through his mind. The Emperor, the richest and most powerful man on earth. The one who had turned him into a freak just because he could. The one he had sworn to get revenge on.

He went to get his gauntlet.

Soon Pryadar was prepared to receive him. The insects on his back were carefully washed away, and his flesh bandaged and dressed.

Seamus Todd came to his cell, the one with the two-way window and recording equipment.

"How are you?"

"I – thank you for my back. I didn't know how much pain I was in until it stopped." He knelt before him, touching his ankles.

"You don't know how much pain you've inflicted on others."

"I do, I do realize. Ever since I took the throne from my father, everything has gone wrong."

"You tried to kill us all."

"And I failed."

The grip on his ankles increased.

"Let me go," said Seamus Todd.

"I'll let you go if you let me go."

The two guards rushed in and beat him back with the butts of their rifles. "I'm sorry, I'm sorry," Pryadar cried.

"You were going to hold me until they did what you wanted."

"No, no. I'm sorry, I really am."

"You're pathetic."

Seamus Todd resisted the urge to throttle him. Looking at the guards, they would not only allow it, they expected it, and would let him get away with it. Here was this Asura, groveling before him like his slaves had bowed before him when he was Emperor. It was disgusting. He expected him to be as arrogant and unapologetic as always. He had at least some grandeur, though of a dark sort. He actually preferred the old, seemingly invincible war lord to this pitiable, simpering fool.

"I know what you are."

"So?"

"I knew your weakness, but I didn't do anything about it. Naganandini confirmed what I had already guessed. I spared you from death. You could at least do the same for me."

"Just because I'm gay, you were going to kill me."

"It's the law. But I didn't want to follow this archaic, foolish old law, simply because I liked you."

"You're liking people is poisonous. You destroy everyone who comes close to you, anyone who tries to love you."

"So do you. It is just one of the many ways we are alike, you and me. You are like my own son I never had."

"You had a son. You mistreated him because he was illegitimate."

"Bastards usually fare far worse in our society. Many are put to death or exiled for the smallest offenses. I kept him as close as I could, risking my throne for him."

Pryadar deserved death. He had done a great deal of damage in his quest for the throne. He had stolen, lied, cheated, murdered to get the throne, then reintroduced slavery and genocide. The world would be a better place without him.

"Look at the beautiful world." Seamus Todd gestured at the window. "A world of green and mist, with castles poking out in the distance. Little villages with lattice decorations."

"You see something I don't when you're looking at it. All I see is the stronghold of my enemies."

They watched the battle together for a while. The Asura armada was putting up a good fight, but they were no match for the Elves in the air. Six more Regime ships were lost. The most important strategy was to keep the enemy along the border, where powerful land-based guns could fire on their ships. Some of the burning ships were trying to crash into targets on the ground.

"What a waste," said Seamus Todd.

"You could surrender, you know."

"We both know that won't happen."

"You're a cruel boy," Pryadar said.

"I'm cruel? Me? You've got a lot of nerve. You're the one who had me tortured, you're the one who. . ."

"None of my crimes were anything to me. I wasn't nearly as bad as I could have been. Do you realize how often I thought of torturing and killing thousands, millions? How often I restrained myself?"

"Your only defense is, you could have been worse? Your imagination is as diseased as your thoughts."

"You hate me because I'm an Asura."

"You're a despicable tyrant. It's not your three heads, it's what goes on in them. And destroying your enemies is nothing everyone doesn't think about once in a while, but you make your atrocities come true."

"You're a racist."

"No, Pryadar, I'm not just like you."

The sky was growing misty with the fume of their exhaust. The green and white ships of the Elves swept over the black and orange ships of the enemy, which were becoming fewer all the time. This time, the Io caught a battleship, and Seamus Todd left to welcome them with his reassurances. Then he returned to the Emperor's cell. The lasers flashed by in what should have been silence, but the ship's audio system picked up the noise and broadcast it to the crew.

His mood had changed again. Now he seemed proudly defiant.

"You plan to kill me. Go ahead, I'm not afraid. I knew you would be the death of me."

"Me?"

"Ever since you said that silly stuff to the Emperor, refusing to flatter him. Ex-Emperor. I knew you were dangerous, but I didn't do enough to stop you. Now it's too late. So, strike me down. You know I, unlike you, won't be returning."

"I forgive you."

"What?"

"I said I forgive you."

"How dare you forgive me? You should be begging me to forgive you."

"For my face?" He started to remove his bandages.

"Well, yes, there's that. But that wasn't really my fault. It was Alexis who did that. I never meant for you to get hurt."

"It was your orders."

"Alexis didn't follow my orders!"

"I forgive you."

He shook his head.

"The disguise falls away, and I am Joseph, your brother."

"I don't understand the reference."

"It's not important. Look. We can make a better world with both our people. We don't have to fight all the time. Strife can be overcome with love. Imagine the intelligence of the Elves with the technology of the Asuras. There won't be anything our two people can't do together. We can build a moon base, we can explore new worlds, and so much more. Join us, Pryadar."

Pryadar said nothing.

"My lord, consider. . ."

"I have. And everything you say repels me. I would rather see the Elves destroyed than compromise my power. What I want most of all is a world ruled by Asuras, conquering and unconquerable. But if I can't have that, I would rid the world of your kind. And if I cannot do that, I would rather blow it up than accept the world the way it is."

"I feel sorry for you."

"I feel sorry for me, too. I was close to achieving my goals, and you stopped me."

"Me? I only played a small part. All the Elves together did much more. But the one who defeated you is yourself."

"I defeated myself? How, may I ask, did I do that?'

"You overreached yourself. You turned your supporters against you. Your own daughter, I'm sure she loved you once. But you turned away her love. Rustem's, too."

"I did love them once, but they don't respect me."

"You didn't earn it. I'm sure they respected you once, but you wasted it. And your men still love you and follow you. They would die for you, why don't you help them?"

Silence.

"Do you want to contact the armada and tell them to surrender?"

"I would."

He brought him the telecommunicator. "It's all set up, you can reach the whole fleet at once."

"This is Emperor Pryadar Bin Harsha. Fight! Fight to the last man. The cause will be the more glorious for the blood of martyrs. . ."

Seamus Todd snatched the communicator away.

"This is Seamus Todd McKenzie. Ships that turn away from the battle and surrender will not be shot at. Lower your weapons and surrender. Enough lives have been lost."

"Don't listen to him," said Pryadar, though he didn't have the microphone and they couldn't hear him. "Get up and fight!"

Some of the ships dropped out of the fight and were escorted to a landing strip on the ground far below. Others fought more furiously than ever, though it was now obvious which side would win. Some of them even tried to shoot their own ships that were surrendering, but the Elven crafts came to the rescue.

"Relax, it's all taken care of. We're trading any Elven hostages taken during the battle for you."

"Thank you, lad."

"They were eager to secure you, safe and alive."

"Who? Hagar Semiramis is dead."

"Your daughter. Naganandini."

"Lad, you don't mean to send me to her, do you?"

"It's all arranged."

"She will kill me."

"Of course, she won't kill you. She's your own daughter. I know things have been a little awkward in the past, but you two are family. About all you have left."

197

"She hates me."

"She loves you."

Don't you remember her swearing to kill me? You were there, lad. She said someday I would kneel before her, begging for my life. And she won't give it."

"A little begging may be all she needs. Let go of your pride, my lord."

The Oath

Not harming civilians or prisoners of war was deeply ingrained in Elvish culture. Seamus Todd was sorely tempted to break it, which would have made him the first in history to break the oath.

"She's going to put me to death. I'm sorry, I don't have extra lives like you do. Asuras live a long time, if we don't die, but once we are dead, that's it. And it means missing out on the centuries I would have had."

"If you're that scared, I'll go with you."

"What? You really mean it?"

"Of course I mean it."

"Thank you, lad. Perhaps she'll kill you and spare me."

"Or spare us both."

"Or kill us both," warned Pryadar.

It was over. Not a single enemy fighter remained. The Io picked up one more pathetic ship on fire, and Seamus Todd welcomed them. Soon, the Io was landing back in Paris, having saved over two hundred and twenty lives.

"I promised the Emperor I would accompany him to Caer Wydr. Please arrange it."

"Yes, lord McKenzie."

"You've become very popular," said Pryadar, a hint of admiration mixed with dismay.

"My people know I trust them. Together, we've achieved great things."

"You really mean it. You're going with me."

"I said I would, didn't I?"

"Thank you."

What was he doing? He was agreeing to hold the hand of an Asura he didn't even like and fall into the clutches of someone he detested. He wondered if snobbishness had more to do with it than compassion. Did royalty deserve any better than anyone else when it came time to die? Having understood compassion better by practicing it, he understood its strength. Still, perhaps he was going too far. Some people didn't deserve pity, and Seamus Todd had already spent as much as he deserved on Pryadar.

CHAPTER TEN

Going Home

Soon a ship was arranged for them, and they took off for the capital. Pryadar trembled the entire way there, but he seemed to relax when he looked at Seamus Todd. Then he would smile nervously.

The endless day continued, though the new star was pulling further and further away. In another two days, night would return to the Earth. In a few months it would be beyond Mars. In a dozen or more years it would look like any other star. Seamus Todd let the warm beams play across him, and he sighed. It was good to be alive.

The truth was, he was almost as worried about facing Naganandini as her father was. He knew she could be dangerous, and guessed she had hysterical personality disorder. But he had made a promise and he was going to keep it. He had learned to value his word.

They arrived at the royal airport. Two large demons were waiting for them. Without a word, they were guided into a vehicle, and took off for the castle. It was a more modern model than the one Seamus Todd and the Emperor Harsha had traveled in, being a flying model. Flight was not allowed inside the shield of the city, but it was also adaptable for driving on the ground.

"What is that?" Asked Seamus Todd.

It was a long line of vehicles, leaving the city and heading in all directions. Over the roar of flying vessels, he could just hear a distant siren.

"Could we turn on the radio?" He took their silence for assent, since the backseat had controls.

"Red alert! Repeat, red alert! The Duchess is threatening to blow the nuclear fusion reactor. All citizens are urged to leave Caer Wydr as quickly as possible. We have a credible bomb threat, and everyone across Europe should take precautions. This is a red alert! Please. . ."

They continued listening, trying to hear exactly what was happening. They were the only ones on the road headed north. He didn't know there was an airship following at a safe distance.

"Oh, no," whispered Seamus Todd. "She's snapped."

"I told you she was crazy and dangerous."

"We have to stop her."

"You'll do nothing," said the demon who wasn't driving. "Our orders are to take the former Emperor to the capital. Her ladyship is waiting."

"I'm the Emperor. I command you to stop."

"We have orders from the new empress. She is now ruler of both Tuatha and the Regime, and you are nothing but an overthrown tyrant."

"Please, we have to stop her," said Seamus Todd.

The demon responded by rolling up the divider between the seats.

Seamus Todd was afraid things had gone very wrong. While the Emperor continued to pound on the glass, he tried to force himself to become calm. They were being delivered like so many packages of meat to a crazy woman. The hostage situation, the tower, the sandstorm in the desert, the crashing ship, he was probably in a worse situation than he had ever been in.

The city was mostly deserted. A few stragglers were still flying away as they drove through the deserted streets. The beautifully crystalline Elven architecture seemed frozen around them, as if trying to warn them away. There was little they could do, though, as doom approached closer and closer.

And there was the castle, rising like a frozen splash of water, or a palace of ice, or a fire suddenly stiff, though it was all crystal.

The Grand Duchess Naganandini greeted them on the steps of the castle. She wore an elaborate gown and cap and was wearing a veil. They were escorted inside, among a phalanx of Demons.

They went down several hallways, up several stairs, into the throne room, with its magnificent balcony. A cage was waiting there, and some kind of machine. Seamus Todd wondered what it was for. Pryadar took one look and turned pale. Apparently, he recognized it.

"I wasn't expecting the Elf. But what a nice surprise. Now I have both of you."

"And what are we here for?" Asked Seamus Todd.

"To see my moment of triumph. The two of you will help in my coronation. Bring me my crown."

Hoping she would be satisfied with that, Seamus Todd played along. They brought her the crown of Tuatha, a many circled band of gold carved with leaves. The ermine cloak, the scepter, the globe, the sword of state.

"I crown thee, queen of Tuatha and the Regime," he winked at Pryadar to take the hint and humor her.

"Here is your cloak, dear," he placed the mantle on her shoulders.

"Your scepter and globe, your majesty."

"The ritual sword, in the hopes that it will remain sheathed and never used."

Then Pryadar opened the ampule of oil and anointed her with it.

"Now I am queen. It is everything I ever dreamed."

"Is that enough?" Asked Seamus Todd.

"Not a chance." She turned on her father. "I swore I would have my revenge on you."

"I offer the Elf in my place. Do anything you want to him, just spare me."

"Why, you. . ." said Seamus Todd. There didn't seem anything more to say. He should have expected treachery but thought Pryadar had learned a lesson. This had been his plan all along.

"Why should I have to trade for him when I have you both?"

"My life is already over. I have you for a daughter, what else could happen to me? His life is more valuable than mine."

"Yes, father," she leaned forward on the throne. "Every life is worth more than yours is. At the moment, an insect, a fly, has a longer life span expectancy than you do."

She left Seamus Todd with the Demons while her father was placed in the cage. "You're just in time for tea." She brought out a set of the finest bone china, decorated with pictures of roses and periwinkles.

She took the tea and poured herself and her father a cup. Then she poured something else from a small vial into his drink.

"Here's your tea, father."

"I can't drink it."

"Do you remember the time I was lost in the tower, father?"

"Yes, I do. I was worried. We were looking all over for you."

"You had no idea I was missing. It was the servants who found me."

"Dear, I had a kingdom to run. I wanted to spend more time with you, but I couldn't. Your grandfather needed someone to run the kingdom for him. I had no choice."

"I have no choice, either, father." She stirred and sipped her drink. "Now, drink your tea."

"I can't."

"Father, I'm giving you a chance. It's either the tea, or the machine. With the tea, you will simply drip off into a sleep from which you will never awaken. The machine," she gestured, "well, you already know what it can do. It's the most agonizing death machine ever built. You designed it."

"Please, Naganandini. . ."

"Drink your tea. Before it gets cold, father." Her voice did not raise.

"You know I can't."

She put down her cup. "No, I suppose you can't."

"Naganandini," Seamus Todd said. "May I say something?"

"No," she said. "Don't waste my time."

"I really think I ought to say something. I know things haven't been all right between you two, but it seems a little extreme to have to try to kill each other."

"If you want him to live, beg for his life."

"What?"

"Beg for his life."

"Please. . ."

"On your knees."

"Elves aren't really good at this," Seamus Todd explained. Slowly, he lowered himself to the floor. "Let's end this. Send him to the Elves for judgment. There's no way he'll be acquitted, give him a life sentence in prison. Imagine being in jail for centuries. It's worse than death, when he's had the life he's led, being the most powerful man on Earth. Feasting on steak and caviar one day, boiled broccoli for the rest of his miserable life."

"You're right, Elves aren't good at this."

"I told you. But you haven't done anything, yet, so why don't you just walk away?"

"You don't know what I've been doing. Prince Jason, come in."

The prince entered, wide saucer eyes unblinking. He noticed the glint of metal around his wrist.

"A zombie," said Seamus Todd.

"There is only room for one on the crystalline throne."

"Let him go."

"Will you take his place?"

Seamus Todd said, "yes, I will. I will marry you. Together, we will rule Tuatha and the Regime, and make it a much better place than it was before. The Regime, I mean."

"Why should your people take the lead?"

The youth replied "because our way has worked, and yours hasn't. We want peace, they want war, but together, we will bring justice and mercy to the throne. Say you will do this with me."

"If I summon a judge, will you go through with it?"

"Yes, anything, only don't blow the reactor."

"I knew you would come around to my way of thinking."

"Wait a minute. I am still her father. Haven't I got something to say in the matter?"

"No," said Naganandini.

"Yes," said Seamus Todd. "We need your blessing if this is going to work. You will rule the Regime directly, we will rule

Tuatha from here, and we will all share in the rewards. It's the perfect idea."

"You seem to be forgetting something," said the Grand Duchess.

"Yes, my dear?" Asked Seamus Todd.

"I promised to kill him."

"That's all in the past. Let's forget about all this nasty business and look forward to a new age of peace and prosperity. . ."

"There can be no peace as long as he's alive. Load him in the machine," she said.

"No!" Said Seamus Todd.

"No!' He tried to struggle, but the Rakshasas held him fast. They opened the hatch and tossed Pryadar, kicking and screaming, into its maw.

"Darling, please."

She said nothing.

"Patricide is not a daughter's crime."

"I'm having it done."

His screams of terror turned to ones of agony. Seamus Todd couldn't see what was happening, but it sounded like he was being flayed alive.

The machine opened. There was an image of the Emperor, his faces a mask of fright. He appeared to have had his flesh replaced by metal. His hands were held out together, holding his golden heart as it burst from, or was torn, from his chest.

"Now at last I can hold you, I'm not afraid of you anymore. Speak to me, Daddy. Have you nothing to say? So still? So cold? So very cold. Hard as steel. You are now on the outside what you've always been on the inside. Aren't you pleased? I have given you a gift that the world might envy."

Seamus Todd caught a glimpse of something moving on the long balcony above. He yanked his eyes elsewhere.

Naganandini took a metal rod (he didn't remember seeing it, but she must have come prepared) and struck the statue. "Did you feel that, Father? Or that? No, you don't feel a thing. You never did. You're no different from how you've always been. A heart of stone. Unbreakable." She lunged at it again, as if she would break it to pieces with the iron bar.

"Naganandini, that's enough."

Instead of stopping, she redoubled her efforts, but the idol stood firm. "I can't break him. Even in death, he has defeated me. Look at that smirk on his face."

The faces seemed to be caught in a moment of horror. His arms were extended to capture his heart as it blew from his chest. He hoped whoever was in the palace was in position by now.

"No, you've won. You defeated him. And you can't afford to be a poor winner. You lower yourself by continuing to fight him as if he's still alive. If you really want to get the best of him, then be a better ruler than he was. End the war."

She said nothing.

"Be more like your grandfather. Rule wisely and well. We'll forget this episode and show everyone what a great queen you can be. You have everything you ever wanted now. So rejoice. The new age can be your age. . ."

He didn't know why that was the wrong thing to say, but it definitely was. Her eyes met his, and her lovely green eyes were like flames. "My age? This age is your age."

"Hey, there's room for all. It's up to you, now. You are queen of three nations, the Elves, the Demons, and the Genies, and you can remake it all in your own image."

"None of them will obey me. The other Demons will not accept a woman."

"The Elves will. The Genies might."

"The Elves will hate me for being a daughter who killed her own father. You know that's true."

"Well, nobody forced you to kill him. You can escape back to Genie Land and resume your role as queen."

"The Demons won't let me."

"You have. . ."

"I have only a handful of loyal Rakshasas. The others all hate me, they won't let me be queen, they'll attack me every way they can."

"You don't know that. I've been among the people, and I think they will accept you."

"That's enough. You don't know anything. I see I have to destroy you, too. You are the one the Elves will look to. You are loved."

"That's because I'm capable of it. Are you, too? Let go of your pride and your anger. Be the queen you were meant to be."

"You must be the next one into the machine. You're too popular, too beloved. The Elves will choose you."

"Not if I tell them I stand behind you."

"It's too late for that. You're next. You must feed the machine. You will be the next to be immortalized. . ."

And the demon on Seamus Todd's right pitched forward and lay motionless. He had stunned him, and he rounded on the next one, who fell. A laser bolt from above had caught him.

"Nobody move." Somebody shouted from above. In the balcony, a half dozen figures appeared, laser guns drawn. People were coming into the room. There was Michael Desmond, Erin, Brendan, his dad Shawn, and several other Elves. Behind them, he saw Shannon, Rustem, Aliyah, and Rory.

Naganandini shrieked and caught Seamus Todd, with a knife to his throat. She backed into the exit behind the throne. Then he was free. She ran, dodging his outstretched hand, which only caught her veil. He was pursuing her down the corridor while his friends battled her Demons.

She was making for the fusion reactor, which powered the entire Elvish realm. It was located in a drum shaped building north of the castle. He hurried as fast as he could to catch up with her.

She reached the reactor room first, but he was right behind her. She grabbed the detonation device, which was attached to an explosive device on the side of the reactor.

"Hah!" She gloated in triumph as she turned to face him.

"Don't do this."

"It may not be as big an explosion as colliding both reactors, but I think it will be enough."

"You're going to kill everyone! Please, don't do this." He looked at the reactor, which was a sphere-shaped device about ten feet around, floating in laser powered gravity.

"Why shouldn't I, with less feeling than you would step on an ant hill."

"I wouldn't step on an anthill. Please, my family and friends are here."

"You killed my family, why shouldn't I kill yours?"

"What?"

"You wiped out my whole family."

"No."

"You killed my grandfather."

"No, I didn't. He died in my arms, but I didn't do anything to him."

"You killed him! You killed Ravana."

"It was one of your henchmen."

"You killed my father."

"You killed your own father," Seamus Todd snapped.

"You knew what would happen."

"No, I didn't. In fact, I assured him it wouldn't. I was wrong, I guess."

"You guess. You killed the Poid."

"I do feel some guilt for his death, but I was trying to save him. He didn't want to be saved," explained Seamus Todd.

"How convenient for you. None of it is your fault, is it?"

"There you go. I didn't kill anybody, but you did. You're the one who destroyed so many lives. It would be better to say you and your family destroyed each other."

"And now I'll destroy you. I will survive my own death to watch my triumph over the Elves," said Naganandini.

"Lady, you're crazy."

"You started all this."

"It's been going on for centuries, with or without us. But our part has led us to this moment. Please, don't do this."

"I'm in too deep. They would execute me for the killing of my father."

"Elves believe in justice. They'd give you a fair hearing."

"It's too late," said Naganandini.

He blinked. Of all the times for his epilepsy to act up.

"Did you hear what I said? The Elves will die, but I will live."

He pitched forward on the floor and lay shuddering.

Her face twisted into a slow, cruel smile.

"Is this the best the Elves could send against me? The world's ugliest Elf, an Elf with epilepsy, and you thought you could take me on?"

She approached until they were almost nose to nose.

"See what my father did to you? He made you into – this. And now. . ." She stood and aimed a fierce kick at his head.

And he caught her foot and tripped her. They rolled together, and he snatched the device. He was up in a flash, the controller in his hand.

"You tricked me!"

"Now let's end this. Come back with me, we'll talk to my grandparents and . . ."

"No. You may have taken everything from me, but I can still choose my own end. And take the whole world with me." She edged toward the lasers surrounding the reactor.

"Don't do it. You'll die."

"I'll never die. I am superior to the Elves. I will live again, as queen. No, as a goddess."

She reached the barrier – and collapsed as if hitting a wall. Her final scream seemed to freeze his blood.

He turned away. The other Elves came into the chamber just then. They were all here. Shawn, Michael, Erin, Brendan, Rustem, Rory, Aliyah, the king and queen.

"I tried to save her. She took her own life."

"And you saved everybody's."

Seamus Todd shook his head. He had seen too much. He just wanted to go home and sleep. He looked around at them all, and noticed Jason was part of the crowd.

"Here, let's take that off you."

He removed the zombie bracelet from his wrist. After a moment, his pupils returned to his eyes, and he was released from the spell.

"Where is my beloved?"

"Naganandini passed away, your highness. I am sorry." He discovered he was.

"Who are all you people?" How dare you! I will take over the Demons. I will avenge myself for the loss of my love. I declare Perpetual War between the Elves and the Demons. . ."

"Grab him," said Seamus Todd, thoroughly filled up with his nonsense. Two guards took Jason on each side and carried him away.

He went to Naganandini's body and gathered her in his arms. Now that she wasn't ranting and raving, she was beautiful and pathetic. He reached down and touched her.

And she let out a gasp.

"She's not dead!"

"Or you revived her."

"It's a very rare Elven skill, but it's not unheard of," explained Michael Desmond. "Seraphs have the power to revive the very recently dead."

"What's happening?" He sank to the floor, suddenly spent.

"That's what I was about to say. You take their injuries on yourself."

"Is there still time to save the Emperor?"

"I don't know if he can be brought back, McKenzie. No one's ever tried it on a petrified person."

"I'm willing to try."

They carried him back to the throne room and laid the statue of the Emperor on the floor. They chipped out his heart and put it back on his chest, and Seamus Todd tried again.

This one was much harder, because the Emperor's body had changed much more than the girl's. He clenched his teeth. Finally, just when he was about to give up, he saw the stone turning soft again. His own hands, though, were becoming steel. He concentrated some more on healing Pryadar's body. Finally, the three headed man choked and set up.

"Why did you revive me?" Asked the Emperor when he could speak. I didn't want another life. I will never be over the pain, nor free from your prison. This is the worst thing you could do to me." Seamus Todd's power wasn't enough to give him back his heart and life. He sank to the floor and died, permanently this time.

"I hate you," agreed Naganandini. "You have given us the worst punishment of all."

"I know," he said, just before he fainted.

Suicide

Naganandini's suicide was honorable by Regime standards. The most usual method is a triple death, where a person takes poison, is beheaded and has their blood spilled from the side at the same time. Fire, hanging, falling on a sword and using a laser gun were also considered honorable. Drowning and death by poisonous gas were considered dishonorable.

"We're ready, your highness." The doctor said, making a final adjustment to the machine.

He walked into the chamber, and a warm golden light fell across his face. Healing. He stepped out again, his face completely restored. He looked in a mirror. He was almost like his former self, but he looked more like an adult than he had.

"Thank you," he said.

Seamus Todd dashed over the hill to the lighthouse. There were his mother and father, his brothers, Thomas and Christian, his sisters, Siobhan and Shannon, and Siobhan's doctor boyfriend, Eric. And Rustem and Rory, Aliyah, Michael Desmond, Erin, Brendan, were all there for him. The sun was fading in the sky. Night was returning to Earth. It was time for a celebration. Seamus Todd's star pulled away, and the stars came out. Since it was the first time they had appeared in three days, their coming evoked awe and wonder in the people gathered to see them again.

Since Jason's abdication, Sean and Caroline had been elected king and queen. They were moving from the lighthouse back to the palace. Rory was going with them, while Aliyah and Rustem were going back to the Regime to help form the new government. Only Naganandini and Jason were left unhappy, as they were all in prison.

It was everything he could have hoped for. The light of the light house went out, a signal that the war was over, then blazed anew, the sign for a new age.

He and Rustem walked along the beach, where he had been digging potatoes when this whole thing started.

"We used to be the same height. Now you're taller."

"Apparently, I am a rare sport called a Seraph. I'm both giant and Angel." He fluttered his wings. It's kind of nice."

"We're free now. The law against us being together has been revoked. Don't you want to come live with me?"

"I would, but I have responsibilities here. I'm going to train to be a diplomat under Michael and Erin. So, it will be a while before I can see you again."

"I'll wait for you. With the law repealed and my mom and new stepdad as president of Arabia, they'll be coming from all over to see me. Thanks to you."

"Then take this ring, as my pledge. We'll get married when we grow up." It was the ring his mother had given him.

"Thanks." They hugged each other.

"Oh, and here's a picture of me, to remember me by."

"Thank you." They embraced. Everything would be all right.

Though they would get back together and eventually unite their kingdoms, let us leave them here, locked in an embrace.

The End.

APPENDIX

All dates refer to the Fifth Age, unless otherwise noted.

A

Aliyah – (5512 -) a Persian princess promised to Prince Ravana. When he died, she married Seamus Todd. After the fall of the Regime, her parents became the monarchs of Persia.

Alexis – (? - 5524) a Demon, major domo to Pryadar. He was killed by Pryadar for killing Seamus Todd.

Amazonians – South America was less severely affected by the alien invasion than some of the northern continents, and the survivors there became the people known as Amazonians or Patagonians. They had a mix of modern, Latin, and native styles.

Asuras – were the offspring of humans infected with the Poid virus. They might have several heads, multiple arms or legs, and any color of skin. They were clearly established within the first century of the Fifth Age, often as rulers over Demon or human populations.

For all their powers, Asuras were never numerous, and their survival depended on mating with humans, which they considered inferior. Crossing of Asuras never resulted in viable births.

After the Poid War, the Asuras settled in hot humid reaches of Earth that were amenable to their culture. Three major sites developed, in India, Central Africa, and Brazil. Harsha's father invaded the Middle East from India and established a kingdom there. Called the Regime, it had an Asura royal house over a demon and human population. In 5525, the Regime collapsed, and subsequent rebellions largely ended the reign of the Asuras. They remained an ever-dwindling people, bereft of power and glory for another century or so before fading away altogether.

Asuras were fully capable of exploiting technology, but they were seldom interested in science or nature for its own sake. They built the Obelisk of Thunder, the largest building on the planet, and equipped their soldiers with spaceships, tanks and advanced weaponry. They were capable of invention, but the Elves continually managed to stay ahead in the technological game. Their most sophisticated designs were reverse engineered from crafts stolen from Elves.

B

Blake – King of Tuatha and husband of Margaret. He resigned the throne to Jason and Naganandini.

C

Caer Wydr – the capital of Tuatha, the palace of glass. Actually made of crystal, it resembled a splash of water in slow motion. The city was also the location of the nuclear reactor.

Caer Wydr was originally the Danish city of Vejan. It was redesigned as the capital of the three kingdoms in 4320.

Celtic Cross – a cross with a circle behind the crux. It was adopted as the symbol of the Elves and appears on their flag.

D

Demons – or Rakshasas, were the result of crossbreeding between Poid infected animals and humans. They served as servants and aides to the Asuras, forming the second highest caste. Asuras could kill Demons, at least their own, without consequence. Demons came in all shapes and sizes, including some attractive ones, but for the most part they were ugly and misshapen. They could not change shape like the Asuras, and though some were winged, none could fly. They could be sneaky and selfish, and plotting against their overlords constantly. Demons turned to stone if exposed to sunlight. That, and their daringness, reduced their already low life spans. A demon died of old age at about eighty to ninety years. The demon who invaded the lighthouse seems to have been Egyptian, but most adopted Hindu culture and dress.

Desmond, Michael – (4037 -) grand old Elf among the ambassadors of Tuatha. In 5524, he agreed to come out of retirement at Queen Margaret's request for one final diplomatic mission to the Regime. Other members of the team included his protegee, Erin, his bodyguard, Brendan Penrod, and his translator, Seamus Todd McKenzie.

Michael survived an assassination attempt while on an airship headed toward the Regime and was unable to complete his mission. His aides tried to take over for him, but they lacked his charisma and experience. After the fall of the Regime and the dawning of the Sixth Age, he retired to his castle in Ireland.

E

Easterners – the people of the East, especially in the lands of eastern Asia. They have dark hair, dark eyes, and high honor.

Elves

Descendants of humans, with virtually immortal lives and diverse abilities. They have pointed ears, and tend toward fair skin, eyes, and hair.

Elves are born one of three types. They are Sprites, Gnomes, or Pixies. Sprites are the largest, like all of them winged and pointy eared, but incapable of flight. Their wings are mainly for display. For their metamorphosis, a Sprite might remain a Sprite, or turn into a Giant or an Angel. Sprites can stun, and some females have sonic powers. Angels can actually fly, and Giants have berserker rages.

Gnomes, or Halflings, are middle sized, between three and four feet tall. They can converse with animals. Those that do not remain Halflings might become Dwarves, which represent the mineral kingdom, or Sylphs, which represent the trees and flowers. Dwarves are between four and five feet tall, slender, beardless, and masters of crafts. Sylphs guard not only the growing things of nature, but the harvests and livestock of other Elves.

Pixies are the smallest of the Elves, between two and twelve inches high. They are capable of flight on their gossamer wings. They transform into Fairies or Brownies. Fairies can heal, and Brownies can hypnotize. So, there are nine types of Elves in all.

Elves live about fifteen hundred years. This is enough for most Elves. After this, aging, which has had little effect on them, begins to catch up. At this point, most Elves choose to end their lives.

Elves represent the arts and sciences. Many Elves are scientists, and almost all practice some form of art, whether it is dance, music, writing, pottery, metal making, painting, sculpting or performing. The ability to create and use powerful weapons like lasers and spaceships, proved decisive in their struggle with the Asuras.

```
        /               |               \
     Sprites          Gnomes           Pixies
     (Stun)          (Animals)        (Flight)
    /      \         /      \         /      \
Angels   Giants  Dwarves  Sylphs  Fairies  Brownies
(Flight) (Warp Spasm) (Mineral) (Vegetable) (Hypnotize) (Heal)
```

The first Elf was Eoh. All Elves are related to him or his companions. The royal family traces its descent from Eoh and Kelsie Heatherton.

Eoh – the first king of the Elves, and the first Elf. He married Kelsie Heatherton in the year One.

In Ten, when the Poid War ended, he led the Elves to Northern Europe, where they settled and crowned him their first king. He ruled until the year One Thousand Ten, and then retired, setting the precedent for long reigns. Elves elect their rulers, usually from Sprites of the royal line. After the arrest of Naganandini, Sean and Caroline McKenzie were elected king and queen.

F

Flags

Tuatha – green, white and blue, with a Celtic cross in the center of the white field.

The Regime – Black and orange, with a horned skull. X shaped pattern.

Kachinas – a green turtle within a sacred hoop on a red, black, yellow and white background.

Genies – The traditional colors of the Genies were blue and gray, and the flag has a gray hawk, the symbol of the Genies, on a white canton on a blue field.

Amazons – a globe of the world on a red and white striped field.

Southerners – Red, gold and brown stripes with a lion as the national symbol.

Easterners – Red Eastern dragon on a gold field.

Australians – kangaroo and emu rampant, holding a shield with the southern Cross, on a white field.

Pacific Islanders – a red green and white hummingbird Dexter, on a blue background.

G

Genies – the people of the Middle East, their eyes and skin turned different colors according to mood. The Regime was built on lands stolen from the Genies, who regained it after Pryadar was dethroned. Genies were unwilling participants in the Perpetual War, but do not seem to have been hostile to individual Elves.

Genies were known for their hospitality. Their lives were shorter than Elves or Asuras, but they lived several hundred years.

Globe – an airship, commissioned in 5509. It bore Michael Desmond and his crew to Neo-Babylon in 5524. It ran under its own power, not from the Elven nuclear reactor. It probably belonged to the diplomatic corps.

Harsha – the second Emperor of the Regime. Harsha was a kindly man, unlike his father and his son that overthrew him. He ruled well and peacefully for eighty years, from 5444 to 5524. Pryadar's forceful taking of the throne was almost a calamity for both Tuatha and the Regime. Exiled, he wandered the world, seeing the state of his kingdom, and died somewhere in Asia Minor. His burial spot is unknown.

I J

Jinns – another name for Genies. Sometimes erroneously used for Demons.

K

Kachinas – the people of North America, descendants of the First Nations. During the Poid War, North America suffered many losses, and the Native tribes, who had fought bravely, were rewarded with their own continent.

L

M

Margaret – Queen of Tuatha before Jason and Naganandini took over.

McKenzie, Seamus Todd – a young Elf, who was chosen to accompany an Elven delegation to the Regime. He was one of the people most involved in the fall of the Regime, and a witness to many of the events that defined the end of the Fifth Age and the beginning of the Sixth.

He was born Aquarius First, 5511. In 5522, his family moved to a lighthouse on the southern coast of Ireland. Their home was invaded in 5524, and he became part of the embassy to the Regime with Michael Desmond.

In the Regime, he was hailed as the incarnation of Prince Ravana, who died while a prisoner of the Elves. He earned the trust of Emperor Harsha and friendship with Rustem, the illegitimate son of Pryadar, but gained the hatred of most of the family. Naganandini tried to challenge him to a duel, which he survived. He was forcibly married to Princess Aliyah, and they made plans to escape together. He was tortured to death by Duke Alexis but returned to life. In revenge, he swore to kill Pryadar, but finally managed to forgive him. He was the team leader of the ship that captured Pryadar, who was traded to the Regime for Elven prisoners. With the election of his parents to monarchs, he became prince of Tuatha.

Macomber, Erin (5495-) Michael Desmond's assistant and protege, she was a beautiful Elf training in the diplomatic corps. Capable of being an ambassador, she was nevertheless rejected by Pryadar as a substitute for Michael Desmond because she was female. She accompanied Brendan and Seamus Todd on the attempt to stop the launch of the fusion reactor ship, and she escaped with Brendan in tow. In the Sixth Age, she was promoted to ambassador to Persia, where she was accepted as fully qualified and an heir to Michael Desmond's proud legacy.

N

Neo-Babylon – largest city in the world, and capital of the Regime. The capital building was the Obelisk of Thunder. Even it was small compared to the massive walls that surrounded the city proper. The walls stood five hundred feet tall, five hundred feet thick, room enough for buildings and a road to be built on it, and enclosed seven hundred square miles.

Naganandini – (5509 -) The only legitimate child of Pryadar Bin Harsha. She overthrew her father and committed suicide, ending the reign of the Asuras. Naganandini might have been a good ruler, but she was selfish, impatient, and angry. Her body was restored after the nuclear fusion reactor incident, and she was sentenced to prison for life for the attempted murder of her father.

Obelisk of Thunder – the largest free-standing building ever built, it was the crowning splendor of Neo-Babylon. Seamus Todd thought it resembled a winged sphinx sitting on a throne.

P

Pryadar Bin Harsha – (5453-) Emperor of the Regime in 5525. He overthrew his father and was murdered by his daughter. Seamus Todd managed to restore him, but he ended up in prison for the rest of his long life.

For much of his life, Pryadar was one of the most powerful and richest men on Earth. He had three heads and six arms. He was born October 31st, 5453 to Emperor Harsha and Empress Zoe, who died giving birth to him. In 5501, his heart condition was diagnosed, and his organ was replaced by a heart plated with gold. He married Naganandini's mother in 5507 and became a father in 5509. A year later, his mistress gave birth to his illegitimate son, Rustem. He married his second wife, Hagar Semiramis, in 5512. They had no children of their own.

He had a brother, who died in a mysterious accident (5509) for which Pryadar was probably responsible. He seemed to have some affection for his nephew, Ravana (5507-5525) but didn't seem to regret the young man's death, which cleared the way for his daughter to become heiress apparent.

He reintroduced slavery during his short reign and tried to conquer and destroy the Elves. When his Ghoul army was defeated by the rising of the new sun, he tried to destroy the fusion reactor, but was foiled by Seamus Todd McKenzie. His next move was to launch a space fleet against Tuatha, but it failed, and he was captured. Pryadar had everything but wasted his opportunities with his selfishness and shortsightedness. He was revived by Seamus Todd and sentenced to life in prison.

Penrod, Brendan (5451-) Giant and bodyguard to Michael Desmond. When his master was injured, he blamed himself, and voted against continuing the mission. He was brave and honorable, but when he was injured during the attempt to seize the fusion ship, Erin was forced to escape with him. After the war ended, he returned to his family in Wales.

Q R

Rashad, Abdul – the yellow robe assassin on the Globe. He fell to his death after trying to kill Michael Desmond.

The Regime – officially, the Golden Land, was the last land ruled by the Asuras. After its fall in 5525, the Asura rule over much of the Earth came to an end.

Rory – friend to Seamus Todd. He was a thief and beggar when they met, but he quickly revealed a steadfast personality. After the fall of the Regime, he moved to Tuatha with his reunited family.

Rustem – Pryadar's illegitimate son. Born in 2511, he fared better than many bastards in that time and place, because of Pryadar's protection. When the Regime was overthrown in 5525, Rustem's mother and stepfather were elected head of the new government of Arabia.

S T

Tuatha – The Elvish Kingdom was formed in 4319 from three smaller kingdoms. The Celtic, Continental, and Nordic Elves agreed to combine their kingdoms by marriage, and their heir would marry the princess of the third. Tuatha was united in 4320.

U

V

W

Wydr – Glass. See Caer Wydr.

X

Y

Z